forgotten TALES of INDIANA

Forgotten TALES of INDIANA

Keven McQueen

illustrations by
Kyle McQueen

The History PRESS

Published by The History Press
Charleston, SC 29403
www.historypress.net

First published 2009

Cover design by Natasha Momberger.

Manufactured in the United States

ISBN 978.1.59629.771.5

Library of Congress Cataloging-in-Publication Data

McQueen, Keven.
Forgotten tales of Indiana / Keven McQueen.
p. cm.
Includes bibliographical references.
ISBN 978-1-59629-771-5
1. Tales--Indiana. 2. Legends--Indiana. 3. Folklore--Indiana. I. Title.
GR110.I6M37 2008
398.209772--dc22
2009035771

Dedicated to Aunt Eulene and Uncle Bob York;
Uncles Bill and Wayne McQueen; and Tayler Fox,
who at age ten is better at fishing than I will ever be.

Contents

Please Take a Bow 9

Rufus Cantrell, King of the Ghouls 11
Monsters and Ghosts 48
Tales from the Tombs 61
Buried Treasure 95
Grave Robbers Galore 100
Life Is Like That Sometimes 117

Bibliography 145
Other Books by Keven McQueen 159

Please Take a Bow

Geneta Chumley, Sandee Clemons, Drema Colangelo, Eastern Kentucky University Department of English and Theatre, Eastern Kentucky University Interlibrary Loan Department, Lee Feathers, Julie Foster, Rosie Garcia-Grimm, Ken Grimm, Kyle and Bonnie McQueen, the Darrell McQueen family, Pat New, the Ossip Fnurd Foundation, Gaile Sheppard, Jonathan Simcosky, Mia Temple, Carol Thomas, Ashley Wray and everyone at The History Press. Also: The Giver.

This book was edited by Lee Feathers of the Green Pine editorial services. www.greenpineeditorial.com.

Rufus Cantrell, King of the Ghouls

We tend to think of body snatching as a problem unique to the nineteenth-century British Isles, but it was a problem in the United States as well. Medical schools needed human corpses in order to teach the fine art of dissection to budding physicians. Executed criminals made good subjects, but there were not enough to go around. As a result, trade was brisk for "resurrectionists" who robbed graves and delivered the dead to medical schools, no questions asked. In 1943, a doctor writing in the *New York State Journal of Medicine* estimated that in the 1840s, "in the City of New York and the surrounding country, not less than six or seven hundred new-made graves were annually robbed of their tenants." By the 1870s, American medical schools dissected about five thousand corpses annually, most of which had been stolen from their graves. Among the prominent universities that participated in the illegal practice were Harvard and Johns Hopkins. Grave robbing was common as late as the 1920s.

The penalties were traditionally lenient because body snatching was considered a "victimless crime"—as long as one was willing to overlook horror-stricken surviving relatives. Eventually, many states passed legislation allowing unclaimed bodies from hospitals and mental institutions to be used as medical subjects. Indiana was one state that had no law allowing an annual quota of corpses for medical schools; as a result, Marion County suffered from an epidemic of grave robbing at the turn of the twentieth century. Cemeteries in Indianapolis and the surrounding area were targeted by organized bands of ghouls.

Since it is the grave robber's business to keep everything looking normal above ground, no one suspected that bodies were missing until about September 1902, when a mysterious man in a closed carriage started making nighttime visits to relatives of the recently deceased. He called himself "the Voice from the Grave." Like a character in a nightmare, he would inform them that their loved ones were missing from their graves and that they could be found at the Central College of Physicians and Surgeons in Indianapolis. Then he would ride away into the darkness. On some occasions, he told people that their relatives were missing by calling them on the telephone, a more mundane but no less disturbing means of getting his message across. His identity was never discovered, but he sowed seeds of doubt and fear among the populace. They took their fears to the police, who later estimated that over one hundred bodies had been stolen within a forty-mile radius in three months, which averages out to at least one grave robbery per night.

Two members of this great army of abstracted corpses turned up at the Central College, just as the Voice from the Grave had promised, on September 17. Detectives were searching for two freshly snatched bodies, those of Mrs. Johanna Stilz and Miss Glendore Gates, stolen from Ebenezer Cemetery and Anderson Cemetery, respectively. The two bodies initially found at the Central College were not those of Stilz and Gates; they were a young black woman named Stella Middleton and Mrs. Rose Neidlinger. Nevertheless, the evidence was clear that the school had been trafficking in illegally obtained cadavers. After detectives made this discovery, it was a simple matter to track down those who had supplied the goods. A gunsmith told police that four black men had purchased rifles from him, with payment guaranteed by Dr. Joseph Alexander, professor of anatomy at the Central College. The authorities felt that this could be more than coincidence, especially since Dr. Alexander had made some foolishly callous statements in an interview with the *Indianapolis News*. When the reporter asked the distinguished physician if he had purchased the corpse of Stella Middleton, Dr. Alexander pled ignorance.

REPORTER: "You would know if you paid out the money, would you not?"

ALEXANDER: "No, I can't say that I would. No questions are asked as to the identity of the persons that deliver the bodies, or the one to whom the money is paid."
REPORTER: "Who brought in the body of the Middleton girl?"
ALEXANDER: "I don't know."

He added with a frankness that bordered on the foolhardy: "We don't care where they [the bodies] come from."

On the morning of September 29, police arrested a gang of seven black men suspected of the graveyard marauding: Rufus Cantrell, Walter Daniels, Solomon Grady, Sam Martin, Garfield Buckner, William Jones and Isham (also given as Isom) Donnell. (Others indicted later were Albert Hunt, Walter and Leroy Williams and William McElroy.) The leader of the gang, Cantrell, quickly confessed and implicated the others. In fact, he said, they had intended to make an excursion to Cherry Grove Cemetery on the evening of the day they were arrested. Citizens probably thought that the nightmare was over; instead, they were only just beginning to confront the darker aspects of human nature most of us would rather not acknowledge.

Cantrell confessed that he and the other six men raided cemeteries while well equipped with the usual tools of the trade: ropes, shovels and horses and wagons for greater ease in carrying away the treasure, and shotguns in case of trouble. The robbers despoiled graves in several local cemeteries, with the exception of the well-guarded and upper-crust Crown Hill. One cemetery, Mount Jackson, located on the outskirts west of Indianapolis, was robbed so often that it was left "practically empty." Cantrell remarked, "We pretty near cleaned that place out. I don't believe we missed any body that has been planted there since July." He later estimated that nearly one hundred bodies had been removed from this cemetery alone. Other locations that proved fertile hunting ground for the ghouls were Ebenezer Lutheran Cemetery, the Indianapolis German Catholic Cemetery, Garland Brook Cemetery at Columbus and the burying ground at the Central Hospital for the Insane. An interesting bit of shoptalk held that it took an average of twenty-five minutes to rob a grave. Such nonchalant revelations earned Cantrell, a former soldier, his lasting nickname: "King of the Ghouls." Incidentally, Cantrell had formerly preached at the Antioch Baptist Church; members claimed that he would preach over a corpse by day and steal it at night.

Some of the stolen bodies were shipped to medical colleges far away, but many were sold to local schools, whose students practiced dissecting the cadavers in anatomy classes. One school in particular—the aforementioned Central College of Physicians and Surgeons—demanded most of Cantrell's peculiar supply. A more thorough search of the premises on September 30 turned up eight more bodies. According to a contemporary news account, "'Rufus' was the password at the medical college, and when it was uttered by the returning ghouls the doors of the college would always be opened without questioning."

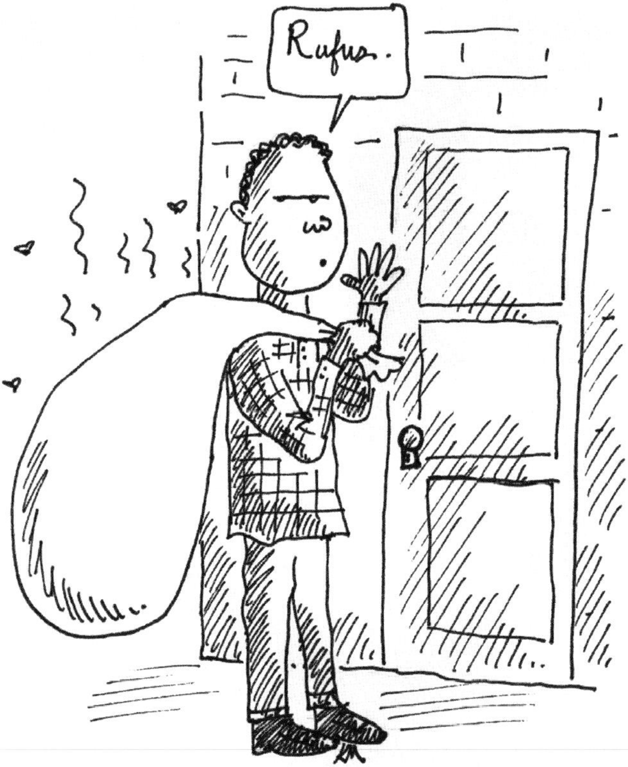

Police had found at the Central College of Physicians and Surgeons ten bodies that had been stolen from their graves, but the remains of Johanna Stilz and Glendore Gates did not turn up. The authorities thought they were simply very well hidden at some medical school, and on October 1 the entire detective force was set to looking for the bodies, accompanied by Cantrell and fellow gang member Walter Daniels. (According to the papers, neither the quick nor the dead were safe from thieves: "Crooks have taken advantage of the heavy work of the police in investigating grave robberies, and today burglaries were reported from all parts of the city.") No additional bodies were found, but a prominent man was arrested that day: Dr. Frank M. Wright, who was on the faculty of the Eclectic Medical College. There was no evidence that he had received a stolen body, but on the other hand there was no evidence that he had not. Indiana law required medical schools to keep careful records on bodies legally obtained for dissection. Breakers of this law faced a penalty of one to three years in prison. Wright had failed to keep records, so off to jail he went. Since no medical schools the detectives searched had kept the required records, Wright soon found himself in good company. Warrants were issued for Dr. David Ross of the Medical College of Indiana, Dr. William Molt of the Physio-Medical College, Dr. John B. Long of the Central College of Dental Surgery and Dr. Edgar Hadley of the Indiana Dental College. The biggest catch of all was yet to come.

On the same day as Wright's arrest, Prosecutor John C. Ruckelshaus questioned the seven members of the grave-robbing gang. They confessed to all charges and implied that many ghouls had not yet been caught. Rufus Cantrell told the police that three gangs of resurrectionists had made Indianapolis their headquarters: his group, another gang of blacks and a third consisting of whites. He refused to name the names of either rival ghouls or his best customers but stated that the gangs had victimized virtually every city and small town in the region, including Anderson, Alexandria, Elwood, Summitville and Fairmount. One rival gang, he said, operated between Indianapolis, Martinsville and Columbus. Some of the bodies were sold to medical colleges in Indianapolis, while most were shipped to Cincinnati and Louisville and then, disguised as bags and barrels containing wholesome freight, distributed to medical schools out west. This was why detectives had found it impossible to find certain bodies.

(The heads of Louisville's medical colleges hotly denied having been involved in the black market cadaver trade, pointing out that legislation passed more than a decade before allowed medical schools plentiful subjects for dissection among unclaimed bodies. The dean of one medical school remarked, "We don't have to steal bodies now"—though the use of the word "now" confirms that they used to. Cantrell's mother later produced a letter of recommendation dated September 12, 1900, written by the faculty at the Central College and "addressed to a prominent city official," proving that the ghoul had in fact gone to Louisville to conduct some business on the school's behalf. Cantrell claimed that he did not do any grave robbing in Louisville because of racial prejudice, but the more likely reason was that the medical schools in that city had plentiful legally obtained subjects for dissection.)

Investigators at local cemeteries confirmed that Cantrell and his gang members were telling the truth. Inspections at Ebenezer Cemetery, Pleasant Hill Cemetery and Jones Chapel revealed that "graves supposed to be untouched had been violated." The graves of the insane had been robbed wholesale at the Central Hospital grounds at Lincoln City. Cantrell said that no body had been left untouched there since 1899. The graves were so shallow that some suspected collusion between the resurrectionists and the staff at the hospital.

Not only the police, but also private citizens headed for cemeteries with shovels in hand to see if their worst fears were to be confirmed. Reports of newly discovered empty graves came daily. Wesley Gates, father of Glendore, went to Anderson Cemetery on September 29 to see if it was true that his daughter's body was missing. (He had been one of the persons warned by the mysterious man in the closed carriage.) When the grave was opened at his request, he and the sexton saw signs of tampering. But since the unearthed casket appeared intact, Mr. Gates refused to look inside and declared that Cantrell was a liar. Perhaps he simply could not bear to find out the truth. The sons of Johanna Stilz had her casket exhumed and found it to contain naught but stale air and a shroud. At Ebenezer Cemetery, the body of Wallace Johnson was officially reported missing. The grave of Mrs. Benjamin Tyler, deceased since November 1901, was opened at Jones Chapel Cemetery; all that was left were a slipper and a couple of tools left behind by the resurrectionists. A happy ending—if you want to call it that—came to Mason Neidlinger, who found his wife's grave empty at Traders' Point Cemetery. The reader will recall that her body was one of the two recovered at Dr. Alexander's Central College of Physicians and Surgeons; Neidlinger had it reinterred encased in a block of cement. Another family determined that resurrectionists who tried to make off with their dearly departed would pay with their lives. On October 22, attorney Jesse E. Hodgin buried his wife at Summit Lawn Cemetery near Westfield and with her "a quantity of nitroglycerin was placed in the grave in such a position that should an attempt be made to open the box containing the coffin it would explode," according to a newspaper account. Hodgin estimated that if the explosive went off it would make a hole in the ground fifty feet square and about fifteen feet deep and would kill anyone near the grave. He acknowledged that the blast would also atomize his wife's corpse, but oh, the moral victory! I suppose the nitro is still down there, making cemetery groundskeepers nervous if they even know about its presence. Meanwhile, the less pyrotechnically minded members of the New Albany Common Council voted to have powerful electric arc lights installed in the Fairview Cemetery and the local black graveyard.

Based on Cantrell's confession and other evidence, the police swore out warrants for, and later arrested, a number of conspirators. By October 14, the ranks of the arrested included nine black ghouls, three white doctors, a black

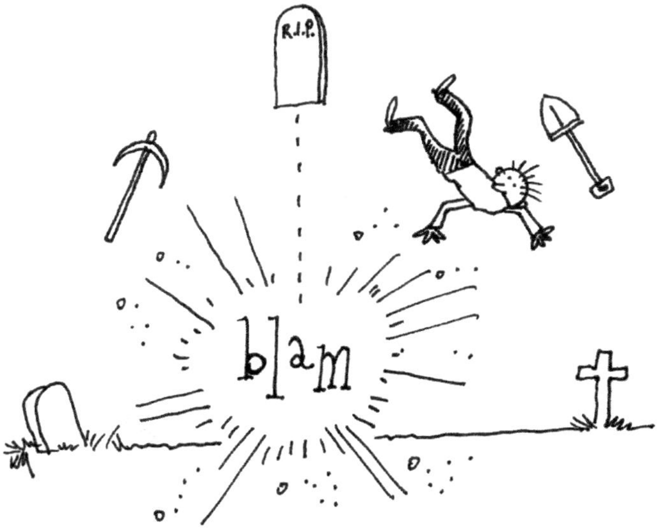

undertaker named C.M.C. Willis (who had formerly employed Cantrell as a hearse driver), a cemetery proprietor named Harry Speers and Speers's night watchmen. The list included three staff members of the Central College: Dr. John C. Wilson of Owenton, Kentucky (an intern whose bail was fixed and signed by every member of the faculty); George Haynmaker, the college janitor; and, by far the most prominent and respectable man to face charges, Dr. Joseph C. Alexander. He was the object of the most public outrage since he played the most active part in procuring the bodies. Cantrell confirmed that the physician had supplied the gang with its shotguns and had paid the then princely sum of thirty dollars for each body in good condition. The robbers were allowed to keep whatever jewelry they found. Cantrell claimed that Dr. Alexander had personally joined the gang when they endeavored to remove from Anderson Cemetery the body of a suicide victim named Dietz. However, since Dietz's grave was topped by elaborate floral arrangements, the robbers left empty-handed because it would have been too difficult to restore the grave to its original appearance. Cantrell confirmed investigators' suspicions that Dr. Alexander had a secret deal going with the proprietors of the Hospital for the Insane, in which hospital officials informed him every time a patient died and intentionally had the graves dug only a foot or two deep. Some bodies were spirited away even before they were buried, and Cantrell said that some graves contained nothing but coffins full of rocks. The disgusted Prosecutor Ruckelshaus told the press: "[E]very man who had a hand in the desecration of graves shall be punished, white or black, prominent or otherwise."

Cantrell, who was twenty years old, seemed to enjoy his newfound notoriety and proudly admitted to anyone who asked that he was the only original King of the Ghouls. "I'm not ashamed of what I have done, and would probably do it again if the police would give me a chance," he told an interviewer. "Grave robbing is a legitimate business, and it's no disgrace to be in it. The best physicians in the city have told me and the others in the gang that the laws were such in this state that we could not be arrested." If the doctors did tell him that, they badly misled him. Cantrell, his gang and the arrested physicians were in serious trouble. They faced long prison sentences because Indiana had strict laws against grave robbery. The penalty for merely disturbing a grave was three to ten years; for removing a corpse, three to ten years; for concealing a stolen corpse, one to three years; for dissecting corpses for which there was no written record of receipt, two to five years.

Cantrell shared details about the practical side of his work. His gang seldom stole the bodies of children because they were "too small" and therefore there was not much demand for them as medical subjects. Ghouls would alert one another if the body within a particular plot was "undesirable" by leaving a lump of coal at the foot of the grave. Sometimes, he and Dr. Alexander would ride around in cemeteries in a carriage looking for recent additions ripe for later plucking. Cantrell's description of the act of removing a body from the grave is well worth hearing in his own words:

> [The other gang members] *dig out the dirt and I look after the rest. When the box is reached then it's my time. I go after the stiff and jerk it out. It's a job everybody can't do…I don't use hooks. I usually get 'em out with my hands. I can do it all right. Once in a long time I find it necessary to use the hooks. If the*

body sticks in the box the hooks are put on and the other fellows help me pull it out.

Finally, Cantrell admitted that he had stolen the body of Glendore Gates. Her father opened the grave a second time, accompanied by reporters. This time, he gathered the courage to look inside the casket and found it empty.

The ghoul's grisly revelations seemed to be endless. He revealed the names of four more people who had ended up as medical school subjects rather than in their alleged graves at Mount Jackson Cemetery: Dorie Snowden, Philip Carter, Albert Tanner and Ed Johnson. He added the darkly comic detail that their bereaved relatives had consigned to the earth coffins containing not bodies but blocks of ice. The cemetery owner, Harry Speers, at first denied that any graves had been robbed. Finally, he confessed that he knew it to be true, but he refused to explain how he knew; on October 11, he and two night watchmen, Adam Ault and Cornelius Jones, were arrested for taking bribes from the ghouls.

On October 7, Cantrell accompanied Detectives Adolph Asch and J.C. Manning to the German Catholic cemetery in Indianapolis. He pointed out at least a half-dozen graves he and his men had robbed, including the plot of Katarina Derringer, who had died six weeks before. Asch and Manning had just enough time to open the grave—empty—when the cemetery groundskeeper informed them that a priest had ordered him not to allow any graves to be disturbed. The detectives returned the next day determined to do their duty and, on the advice of Cantrell and ghoul Walter Daniels, inspected the grave of Catherine Doehring in the presence of her two sons, John and Frank. "A foot or two below the surface excelsior [wood shavings] was found, and the ghouls smiled grimly," wrote a reporter who witnessed the ghastly scene. The casket contained only a Catholic charm and a pin. The reporter described another dramatic scene that unfolded in the graveyard:

> *A patrolman* [who] *had followed the party to the cemetery walked up to Cantrell and said: "Rufus, the body of my mother is buried over there. Is she gone?" Cantrell walked to the grave. He stated positively that the body had not been disturbed. Cantrell offered to prove his assertion and dig open the grave, but the patrolman said he would accept the grave robber's word.*

About a month later, the detectives took Cantrell to the Ebenezer and Anderson Cemeteries to have him point out rifled graves. At Anderson, Cantrell pointed out about forty burial sites that had been robbed by either his gang or rival ghouls. With pride, he led the detectives to the graves of a mother and daughter, both of whose bodies he had snatched—the former with the blessing of her husband, who was willing to look the other way as long as Cantrell gave him half of the thirty dollars a physician paid for the corpse. The cemetery sexton who was present during this confession got a scare when Cantrell admitted that he had tried and failed to steal the body of the sexton's father.

Rufus Cantrell was not the only member of the gang with disgusting stories to tell. Isham Donnell, at least, knew firsthand the pain that trafficking in cadavers could bring to surviving family members. When his own wife had died, he had paid thirty-five dollars for a funeral, only to find that Cantrell and an undertaker (probably C.M.C. Willis) had sold the body to Central College. They had never even troubled to bury it. Friendship is a sacred thing, but business is business.

Meanwhile, Cantrell's statement about there being a rival gang of white ghouls was proved correct. The police received an anonymous tip that the gang had plundered Beaver Cemetery, three miles from Fisher's Station, Hamilton County, taking with them the mortal remains of Newton Bracken, Ida West, Mrs. George Lowe, George Weaver and a boy named Walter Manship, among others. The gang's leader was John McEndree, who was arrested in Martinsville on Halloween. But compared to Cantrell, McEndree was small fry, as his gang had made only about twenty grave-robbing expeditions.

The flush times for resurrectionists were over. Hard-pressed ghouls and medical school faculty suddenly found themselves with a surplus of corpses that they had to get rid of quickly before the law caught them. Therefore, bodies began turning up in exotic and inappropriate places. One stolen cadaver was hidden in a saloon for two days before it was found. On October 4, the indefatigable detectives Asch and Manning raided the Medical College of Indiana. Six corpses in a vat were accounted for in written records, but the detectives found ten unidentifiable, illegally acquired bodies buried in the cellar and covered with quicklime in an attempt to destroy them. The proprietors of the Central College of Physicians and Surgeons knew that they were under suspicion of buying corpses illegally; their janitor, an intern and a top-ranking member of the faculty, Dr. Alexander, seemed destined for jail. Perhaps out of fear, the staff did something really dumb: they attempted to get rid of the remaining evidence by leaving it in plain sight on the streets, hoping to make disposal of the corpses the city sanitation department's problem. On the morning of October 13, a pedestrian walking near the Central College noticed a large sack sitting on top of a dry goods box on the sidewalk. The sack contained something of humanoid shape. The citizen called the police, who opened the sack and found a female corpse inside. Upon closer inspection, they found three more body bags, one inside the dry goods box and two by the rear door of the Central College. Johanna Stilz, Glendore Gates, Wallace Johnson and Catherine Doehring had been found.

On October 25, the grand jury issued twenty-five indictments against the grave robbers and their employers. Five physicians were arrested on October 27: Dr. J.C. Alexander, Dr. William Molt, Dr. Charles Byrkitt, Dr. John

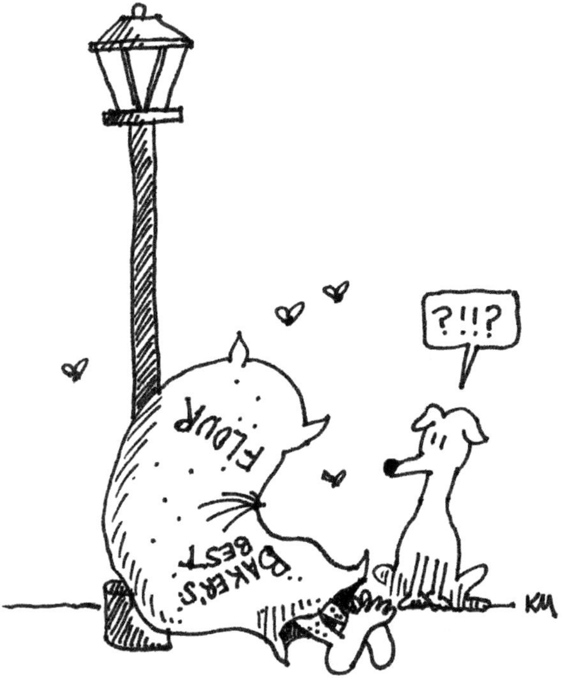

C. Wilson and Dr. Frank M. Wright. But the doctors had money to pay their bonds, ranging in sums from $1,000 to $3,000, and were free to go. Ditto for the cemetery workers. In fact, the only indicted persons who had to return to prison were Cantrell and his gang, none of whom could afford to pay his bail—and all of whom pled not guilty. Slowly but surely, a change came in Rufus Cantrell's demeanor because it began to dawn on him that the physicians who had promised to help him out of his scrape were interested only in saving their own necks.

With exquisite timing, the day before Halloween Cantrell told a reporter that he would turn State's evidence and all the awful things that he had revealed so far were just the icing on a horrifying cake. He had been holding back, he said, because he thought the doctors would give him aid; now that it was obvious they would not, he and fellow ghoul Walter Daniels saw no purpose in protecting their former employers. He bitterly promised that when he spoke before the grand jury, he would implicate fifteen more physicians and undertakers, a couple of female embalmers and some medical colleges and dental schools that had hitherto escaped notice. Cantrell was so serious about helping the prosecution that on November 12, he even turned in one of his jailhouse visitors, William Moffitt, as a grave robber. In a scene reminiscent of a stage melodrama, Cantrell identified his elderly business rival by a scar on his back, received four years earlier when a security guard took a shot at Moffitt while he had been attempting to pilfer a cadaver from the Insane Hospital cemetery. Moffitt had been employed as a janitor at a medical college and allegedly had been a ransacker of tombs for a quarter of a century.

The King of the Ghouls's announcement that he would help the prosecution had some effect because on November 20 Cantrell told his lawyer, Cass Connaway, that a person whom he refused to name had offered to pay his bond as long as he left Indianapolis and never returned. Cantrell refused to consider the offer unless the other members of his gang were given the same deal and, in any case, said Cantrell, "he would not leave the city even if released, as he intended to stay and assist in the fight for the prosecution of the white men concerned in the trouble." To prove his point, at the end of the month, Cantrell positively identified another white man, George Mason, as a member of a competing gang of ghouls.

The prosecution certainly seemed to have what we would now call a "slam-dunk case," but a problem arose. Their star witness lost his zeal for seeing justice done. On January 7, 1903, Cantrell sent a copyrighted letter to a local paper in which he stated that he would refuse to testify against the doctors, cemetery keepers, fellow ghouls or anyone else. Cantrell had decided that he would plead guilty and take his punishment solo. "His declaration means the end of the grave robbing prosecutions, for Deputy Prosecutor Benedict declared…that without Cantrell, the state can do nothing," remarked one newspaper.

Despite this major setback, the prosecution carried on. The long-anticipated trial of the dapper Dr. Alexander began on February 2. Thirty-eight men besides Dr. Alexander were under indictment. The community was so outraged by the grave robberies that a collection was taken up to help defray the costs of prosecution. Among the evidence against the doctor were a couple of shrouds found in the basement of the Central College. One, identified by the woman who had done the needlework, was the shroud of Catherine Doehring. Rufus Cantrell testified on February 4, telling the court that the good doctor "hired him to lead the gang of grave robbers, agreed to pay thirty dollars for each corpse, [and] arranged for vehicles." He had also provided his hired ghouls with pistols, but at least the follower of the Hippocratic Oath had instructed Cantrell's men to shoot "only when necessary."

Another witness, Sam Martin, was a member of Cantrell's gang. He testified that Dr. Alexander had told him in June 1902 that he wanted seventeen to twenty corpses for dissection and would pay thirty dollars a head. The doctor would check the returns at the county Board of Health; whenever he learned of a recent death, he passed the information along to Cantrell. Martin was hazy about dates and unable to remember the specific names of the deceased he had helped steal, but he did recall that the bodies were taken to the Central College of Physicians and Surgeons. Another witness, a liveryman named Case, corroborated Cantrell's statement that Dr. Alexander paid for the rigs used by the gang. W.H. Nickerson, a justice of the peace, testified to having seen Stella Middleton's body on a table at Alexander's school, although her remains were supposed to be safely housed in a grave in Mount Jackson Cemetery.

Witness William Jones did not personally rob graves but had been hired by Dr. Alexander to be the gang's driver. Jones agreed with Cantrell that on one occasion

Dr. Alexander had joined his team of resurrectionists on a trip to Anderson Cemetery. Jones had been present when Wallace Johnson was stolen from the Ebenezer Cemetery; Johnson's remains did not look very spruce, possibly because he had been killed in a train accident—Jones's share of the profits was only five dollars. In the same graveyard, the men pilfered the mortal remains of Johanna Stilz. She was in better shape than Wallace Johnson, and Jones got eight dollars for his trouble. The next project was in the Insane Asylum cemetery; this was followed by a journey to a graveyard near Traders' Point early in August 1902, where the ghouls left with Rose Neidlinger. The next day, Jones testified, he saw Dr. Alexander pumping embalming fluid into Neidlinger's body at the college.

The next witness was gang member Walter Daniels, who was introduced to Dr. Alexander in July 1902 by Rufus Cantrell. Daniels had had previous experience in his peculiar line of work, having found anatomical specimens for Thorton J. Barnes, anatomy professor at Northwestern. Daniels testified that he and Cantrell had stolen the body of Stella Middleton. Spirited cross-examination by the defense failed to shake Daniels's story. When Dr. Alexander took the stand on February 10, he admitted that he had bought some corpses from Cantrell and his men, but made the risible claim that he hadn't known that the bodies were stolen.

In addition to all of this, the witness stand became a site where horrifying tales were related that would have made Edgar Allan Poe's fortune several times over.

Various persons told stories of finding the bodies of family members crammed into barrels at the Central College; of a soiree held for members of high society, where the dancers were blissfully unaware that underneath the ballroom floor "cadavers were piled like firewood"; of bodies being shipped away in laundry machines; of a fight that had occurred in the dark of night between two bands of corpse stealers in the Beaver Cemetery in Hamilton County, during the course of which a marauder named Gray was killed and his body hidden in the conveniently opened grave. Cantrell also told a story about a father who had buried a dynamite cartridge at the head of his daughter's grave in order to thwart grave robbers. Cantrell, refusing to be thwarted, had simply opened the foot of the grave and pulled the girl's corpse out by the legs. For this act of daring, he had been paid an additional ten dollars. On one especially memorable occasion, Cantrell violated a grave only to find that it was his girlfriend's would-be resting place; she had died suddenly and had been buried without his knowledge. I assume that he stifled his sentimental feelings and got his standard thirty bucks.

Arguments by Dr. Alexander's defense began on February 10. There was little his attorneys could do in the face of such overwhelming evidence except: 1) offer character witnesses; 2) let the doctor claim under oath that he had had *no idea* where all those bodies he purchased were coming from; and 3) claim that Rufus Cantrell was both insane and an epileptic and, therefore, his word should not be taken seriously. (Were the other grave robbers who testified that they were in Dr. Alexander's employ also insane epileptics?) The case went to the jury on February 13; as the jury deliberated, according to one account, "an excited young man in the corridors of the courthouse, whose family had suffered by the depredations of the ghouls, declared that Alexander would receive a bullet in the head if the jury acquitted him."

The stunningly lame defense strategy worked. After applying all their gray matter to the case, the jury members announced on February 15 that they could not reach a decision. Dr. Alexander would have to be retried. Rufus Cantrell spent the month of March testifying before a grand jury in Noblesville, Hamilton County, about yet another gang of ghouls who operated there. (One wonders whether grave robbing was Indiana's chief industry a little over a hundred years ago.) Over the previous eight years, virtually all of the thirty cemeteries in the county had been robbed, said Cantrell, who testified that the cold cargo was packed on boats and floated down the White River to a waiting market among the medical schools of Indianapolis. The towns in Hamilton County where cemeteries were robbed included Eagletown, Carmel, Fisher's Station, White Chapel, West Liberty, Sheridan, Cicero, Atlanta and Arcadia. Only Marion County had been the scene of more body snatching. As a result of his testimony, eleven persons were indicted and six true bills were returned. While in Noblesville, Cantrell made extra money by selling photographs of himself.

On March 19 came the first hint that Cantrell's gang had been indulging in an even worse activity than robbing graves. A Chinese laundryman named Doc Lung had been decapitated in his shop on Indiana Avenue in Indianapolis in 1902. A prosecutor named George Spahr suggested that Cantrell knew something about it that he wasn't telling. About a week later, the King of the Ghouls revealed that the killers of Lung were Nim Davidson, a man named Brooks and others including an unnamed Chinese person. Davidson and Brooks were arrested; the latter made a complete confession. In mid-April, Davidson, Ollie Sanders and James Andrews were indicted for the murder; for unknown reasons, Brooks's name disappears from the case. In May, Davidson was sentenced to prison for manslaughter.

Dr. Alexander was scheduled to go on trial a second time on April 13, 1903. But Prosecutor Ruckelshaus announced that his trial had to be indefinitely postponed because Cantrell refused to testify and the other members of Cantrell's gang had decided to follow his lead. Said Ruckelshaus, "We have no witnesses against him. If after these men are tried and convicted they then want to testify they may do so and Dr. Alexander will be tried. If not, Dr. Alexander can never be tried." As Ruckelshaus's statement implies, the members of the grave-robbing gang could still be tried on individual charges of desecrating graves, concealing corpses and the like. It was said that several doctors had bankrolled Alexander's defense in their own self-interest, and the rumor spread that Cantrell and his men were bribed or threatened into not testifying against the prominent physicians. The grand jury vowed to investigate, but I have been unable to discover whether the stories had any foundation. Cantrell, indecisive as ever, told the press, "It seems to me that the best thing for me to do is to be tried and serve out my time in the penitentiary. That's what I think I'll do now, but I may change my mind."

At the same time that Dr. Alexander's case failed to come to trial, a movement was underway to hold an insanity commission on Cantrell. One of his attorneys argued that "an effort was being made to 'railroad' Cantrell to the insane asylum so that he could not appear as a witness against Dr. Alexander." Prosecutor Ruckelshaus retorted that the argument could work both ways: "I have a right to see that no man is railroaded to the insane asylum instead of getting his just dues for crimes committed against the state." When Cantrell finally went to trial in criminal court on April 20, he pled not guilty due to insanity, so his lawyers must have decided that it wasn't such a bad idea after all. (They may have been influenced by the fact that only three days before, fellow ghoul Sam Martin had been found guilty of robbing the grave of Johanna Stilz and was due to be sentenced to three to eight years in prison.)

The defense called in doctors who testified that Cantrell was insane—that he had been mad from childhood, that insanity ran in his family, that he was epileptic, that he had received a spinal injury at age nine, that he had had sunstroke once and that he suffered from a debilitating disease that "destroys the intellectual powers." The prosecution countered with equally convincing testimony from physicians that he was not insane. The prosecution won the day, and on April 23, the special judge—whose name, delightfully, was Charles Coffin—found Cantrell guilty of stealing the body of Rose Neidlinger, with a penalty of three to ten years in prison, and of entering a conspiracy to commit a felony with Dr. Alexander, with a penalty of two to fourteen years in prison. At bare minimum, he would have to serve three years, but his sentence might be reduced depending on his behavior in prison. Since the ringleader of the ghouls had been found guilty, the attorneys for the other gang members advised them to plead guilty and take their lumps. One of the ghouls, Isom Donnell, a cousin of Cantrell's, made a memorable statement when the judge sentenced him to one to three years in the state prison at Michigan City. When the judge noted that Cantrell was being shipped off to a different jail, Donnell wearily remarked, "I've seen too much of Cantrell already."

On May 2, Cantrell began his sentence at the Jeffersonville Reformatory, where he was assigned to hard labor in the physically punishing foundry where he manufactured pots and kettles, much to his disappointment, for he had expected to work in the institution's kitchen. At this juncture, Dr. Alexander leaves the headlines for good. Since no one would testify against him, he was never punished, at least not in a practical sense. A group of indignant Indiana farmers managed to express their contempt by building a scaffold, from which they hanged and burned effigies of the judge and Dr. Alexander.

For now, we must let the prison doors clang shut behind Cantrell and allow him to brood in his cell for a couple of months. *Why*, he must have wondered, *should my cronies and I go to prison for years and everyone else get off scot-free?* In July, Cantrell once again decided to go public with his inside knowledge of the ghouls' activities in hopes of having his sentence reduced—and this time he played a hand entirely made up of trump cards.

According to Rufus Cantrell, he and his gang took a cue from the legendary Scottish resurrectionists, Burke and Hare: whenever trade was slow, they turned living, healthy people into saleable corpses. On July 9, he admitted that he and an accomplice named William Harris had murdered a policeman named Watterson in 1896, Cantrell's first murder. Two days later, he confessed an even worse crime to prosecutor William Long.

On the night of March 11, 1900, a forty-three-year-old schoolteacher from a wealthy Indianapolis family, Carrie T. Selvage, escaped from her room at the Union State Hospital, a private sanitarium for mental patients, clad in a dark blue flannelette wrapper and black felt house slippers. She vanished into the cold darkness outside and was never seen again despite weeks of frantic searching by her family. Her disappearance was regarded as a minor mystery in Indiana, but Cantrell claimed to have the answer. He said that as Miss Selvage wandered down a country lane that night, she crossed paths with Garfield Buckner, William McElroy and Cantrell himself, all on their way home from body snatching. They persuaded the mentally incompetent woman to climb into their buggy and drove away. The gang held her captive in a physician's barn in Hamilton County for fourteen weeks. The press noted, "The most revolting details of her treatment there are withheld by the police." Later, the ghouls moved her to the abandoned basement of an old medical college in Indianapolis with the intention of eventually selling her body, but when the search for her came too close for the gang's comfort, one member chloroformed her, cut her throat and buried her body in Union Chapel Cemetery in a grave whose original occupant they had evicted months before. Cantrell claimed to know the exact location of the body, but refused to say more.

His story got investigators' undivided attention. On July 13, they took Cantrell to the cemetery near Nora, eleven miles from Indianapolis, and asked him to find the body. Once at the scene, Cantrell's memory failed him. He selected two graves and instructed authorities to open them, stating that the correct grave would contain a broken rough box and that the coffin within would have an upside-down lid. Digging revealed that in one grave the lid of the box containing the coffin was standing on edge and the coffin lid was in the position Cantrell described. The body of a woman was found within, but it was so decomposed that Carrie Selvage's brother Joseph did not recognize it as her. Mr. Selvage came away unconvinced that it was his sister, but he believed that Cantrell did know something about her disappearance. The disappearance of Miss Selvage was declared solved, though positive evidence that her body was found was not forthcoming. As late as December 1915, Cantrell, then living in Detroit, stuck to his story, claiming that the murderer was his ex-friend Edward Gowdy.

(The mystery of Carrie's whereabouts took an even stranger turn on April 26, 1920, twenty years after she vanished. Workmen tearing down the old Union State Hospital found a skeleton in a sitting position in a corner of the attic. The skeleton wore a blue dress and black slippers, which convinced Carrie Selvage's three surviving brothers that it was their long-missing sister. Coroner Robinson found no evidence of violence. The grim discovery raised more questions than it answered: Was it really Carrie Selvage's skeleton? If so, had she been brought to the attic against her will or had she hidden there and starved to death? How had twenty years' worth of hospital employees failed to notice her decaying body? Had Rufus Cantrell simply lied about the fate of Carrie Selvage or had the grave robbers—who seemed to have unquestioned access to medical schools and hospitals—managed to plant her body in the hospital from which she had disappeared, perhaps out of fear that they were about to be caught and finding her corpse too well-known to sell?)

Cantrell provided police with information on two more murders. In 1902, five men, including Cantrell, had shot Officer Isaac Rosengarten as he attempted to arrest them for burglary; they then made it look like suicide. The plan almost worked, but the coroner noticed that the bullet in Rosengarten's head did not match the bullets in his revolver. The same men, he claimed, shot to death John B. Stout on Senate Avenue, Indianapolis. Cantrell implicated himself in the murders but was promised immunity if his evidence led to the arrest of the other killers. Cantrell also claimed to know what had happened to Kenneth Lawrence, a wealthy young man from Bellefontaine, Ohio, who had inherited $400,000 worth of property in Indiana and Illinois and who disappeared in New York. These five murders had been extraneous activities unconnected with Cantrell's grave-robbing enterprise. On August 10, the nation's press reported: "[D]etectives are unearthing additional details that corroborate the Negro's statement and point to further startling developments within the next few days."

When Cantrell finished confessing, a wealthy Hamilton County farmer was under indictment for complicity in grave robbing and some Indianapolis physicians were accused of helping murder people for dissection purposes. His harrowing tale of Carrie Selvage's abduction was corroborated; the unfortunate madwoman had escaped from her captors and was seen by an eyewitness before the gang recaptured her. The witness was an acquaintance of Rufus Cantrell's who had already seen him commit a previous murder. When the witness next saw Carrie Selvage, she was dead with a slashed throat and bound in a sack in a basement on North Street frequented by Cantrell and his gang members. Further substantiation came from fellow convicted ghoul Sam Martin, who stated that Cantrell had headed not only the gang of grave robbers but also a gang of freelance murderers called "the Sign of the Cross," named for the symbol members used when signing notes of warning to one another or when arranging details of upcoming homicides.

Indianapolis police spent several days ferreting out and arresting gang members named by Cantrell and Martin, specifically Garfield Buckner, Ollie Sanders, James Gibson and William Hartman. Buckner was wanted for his part in the abduction and murder of Carrie Selvage and the slaying of Officer Rosengarten. Ollie Sanders had already been arrested since Cantrell claimed that he was one of the murderers of the laundryman Doc Lung, but when Sanders turned State's evidence he was released on bond and took the opportunity to flee. He was wanted for the murders of Carrie Selvage and Wallace Johnson and also for crushing the skull of Richard Jordan with a club in a rear yard on North Street to steal his money. James Gibson and William Buckner, according to Cantrell and Martin, were among the murderers of Officer Rosengarten, with Buckner being the trigger man.

Acting on Cantrell's advice, on August 11 the police found a man who had witnessed Jordan's murder but who had been too terrified to step forward; they also found another man who had transferred Johnson's body from the North Street hideout to the medical school where his corpse was exchanged for cash. Clubbing apparently was the gang's favorite *modus operandi*. Cantrell claimed that they also killed a stranger from Pennsylvania named Claude (or Clyde) Brooks (or Johnson), or some combination thereof. After robbing the corpse of $200, they sold it to the Indiana Dental College. He must have been killed about the same time as the murder of Carrie Selvage because a witness saw both bodies with their skulls bashed and their throats cut in the North Street cellar.

The police decided to explore the infamous cellar; there, they unearthed two more bodies on August 12. One was a woman with a slashed throat who was never identified. The other was Walter Johnson of Newark, New Jersey, murdered for $400 in 1900. William McElroy Jr. was promptly arrested and confessed that his father had committed the murder. Rufus Cantrell had driven Johnson to the murder site in Mount Jackson, a suburb of Indianapolis. All five men present were toting clubs; they even let Johnson carry one to allay his suspicions. On a prearranged signal, William McElroy Sr. crushed Johnson's skull with a single blow. The gang sold the body to the Central College the next day. (Did the surgeons notice that they were receiving an unusual number of bodies with cut throats and pulverized craniums, or did they find it more expedient not to ask questions?) The elder McElroy was arrested on August 13 and confessed. The police made a lucky find in Abraham Silberstein, a tailor who had cleaned bloodstains out of Cantrell's clothing soon after the murder of Johnson. They also discovered that the day after Johnson's murder, Cantrell and Garfield Buckner went to Franklin, Indiana, and indulged in a five-day spending spree.

In addition, detectives thought that Buckner, Cantrell and Sam Martin had killed one person in Chicago and alluded to four more murders committed by Cantrell and/or his gang. The final tally, as best as the police could figure: between January 1900 and January 1902 the Sign of the Cross was responsible for about twenty murders. Yet not everyone believed that Cantrell was a reliable witness, despite the wealth of detail he had provided about sundry crimes. He allegedly told an Indianapolis reporter that he had served as the lookout when a couple of accomplices called "Faithful Tom" and Harris murdered and robbed an elderly man named Wilson, proprietor of a secondhand bookstore, in Philadelphia in August 1897. On September 30, 1903, a couple of Philadelphia detectives visited Cantrell in his cell at the Jeffersonville Reformatory and interviewed him. Contrary to the newspaper story, Cantrell claimed that while he knew Harris, he did not know Faithful Tom; furthermore, he denied that he had ever told such a tale to the Indianapolis papers. In addition, the only witness to the Wilson murder claimed that the perpetrators were white. The detectives decided that Cantrell was lying and went home.

Cantrell made so many confessions that he finally became a nuisance and the authorities cut off his speaking privileges. Inmates at the Jeffersonville Reformatory were not allowed to remain after their thirtieth birthday, so on November 6, 1903, Cantrell was moved to the Indiana State Prison at Michigan City—partly because he had reached age thirty and partly because at the reformatory he had "been such an attraction for the other inmates." It is to be assumed that this was not a good thing. Cantrell's richly ironic new job assignment at the prison was to make tombstones, in the same manner that jailbirds today manufacture license plates. It was erroneously reported in June 1904 that the King of the Ghouls was dying of typhoid; I wonder if he contemplated while on his sickbed the prospect that someone might snatch his body from the prison cemetery.

The darkest evil may inspire some good. Public outrage in the wake of the grave robbery and murder scandal led Indiana legislators to update the statutes on subjects for dissection. Physicians argued that so few specimens were provided by the current law that the medical schools were forced to make a difficult choice: either break the law by conspiring with body snatchers or turn ill-prepared young doctors loose in the world. Starting in 1903, medical colleges in the Hoosier State were legally given a certain number of unclaimed bodies of paupers for dissection.

But what happened to Rufus Cantrell, the man whose nefarious exploits led to greater benefit for humanity even if such was not his intention? In June 1905, he was denied a parole despite efforts to remain on his best behavior. By then, two of his accomplices had been freed. Perhaps because his confessions led to the solutions of so many crimes and the arrests of so many criminals, after serving six years he was paroled in May 1909 by Governor Thomas Riley Marshall "on the condition that he secure employment and keep away from Indianapolis." Most, if not all, of his grave-robbing cohorts had already been pardoned. He made the headlines again around Christmas of that year when he applied for a license to marry Hattie Patterson. I wonder what she thought of the nickname the *Fort Worth News* gave her: "Grave Robber's Bride."

Cantrell moved to Anderson, Indiana, where he worked at a steel mill, the owners of which reported his conduct to the parole board. He no longer took pride in being the King of the Ghouls. When in early 1910 he was involved in a family fight that was serious enough to warrant police interference, Cantrell begged the officers not to report his name to the papers or mention his prior record, declaring that he was "trying to live down his past."

But every man has his price, and a grave robber's is probably quite cheap. In August 1910, Cantrell accepted an offer to go onstage at a local vaudeville house, billed as "Rufus Cantrell, the Famous King of the Ghouls." It was further announced that "three other members of the famous ghouls will appear." One shudders to contemplate a Three Stooges–style knockabout vaudeville act involving picks and shovels, but actually Cantrell delivered "a great lecture on his past terrible life."

Later, he made a more serious effort to reform. He attended Booker T. Washington's Tuskegee Institute, where he studied medicine and theology. As Reverend Rufus Cantrell, he became pastor of a 1,400-member Baptist church in Indianapolis; he was dismissed in 1912 for taking the side of liquor men during a Prohibition dispute. Undaunted, he moved to Elyria, Ohio, where he was employed at the Toledo Asphalt Paving Company. He held revival services in June 1913 in an attempt to start his own Baptist church. His services attracted both white and black parishioners; many of the latter traveled from Cleveland to hear him preach. Perhaps Reverend Cantrell's take on the Resurrection was of special interest.

Monsters and Ghosts

Monsters on the Loose

The good people of New Conner, near Muncie, received an unwanted Christmas present in the form of a howling monster that haunted the forests. The creature's presence became known in mid-December 1883 when raccoon hunters' dogs picked up its scent and pursued it. The hunters joined the chase but were increasingly apprehensive as it became obvious that the unseen quarry at the end of the trail was neither fox nor coon. At last, the dogs began circling a hollow tree—but at a distance, as though they were afraid of whatever they had trapped. This so unnerved the hunters that they lost their courage and fled the woods, dogs at their heels. As they ran, an unearthly scream issued from the tree that sounded like nothing they had ever heard. Not long afterward, people began seeing tracks in the snow of an unidentified creature. Something started feasting on farmers' pigs and sheep. Then, rural folk had their hard-earned slumber disturbed nightly by the howls and shrieks of their unknown tormentor. On December 23, John Beals was returning home late at night in a sleigh, like a character in a Robert Frost poem. Unlike a character in a Robert Frost poem, Beals encountered a monster standing in the middle of the road. It dropped a goose that it had been eating and retreated screaming into the woods. As of December 27, there was talk of forming a search party to find the beast—but, as there were no follow-up stories, it is possible that either the monster moved elsewhere or the locals had second thoughts about forming that posse.

In February 1889, people living at Brushy Ridge, near Columbus, swore that they had seen a critter the size of a red fox, only equipped with wings as well as legs. Like the thing that had terrorized New Conner six years before, this animal was nocturnal and enjoyed entertaining people with its screams.

Anderson was the scene of havoc wreaked by a creature described as being six feet long and with a head like a panther's, but with stumpy legs and a bushy tail. Starting in mid-August 1902, the animal killed pigs, cattle and two horses. At the end of the month, Joseph and Kate Johnson were riding in a buggy when the thing attacked their horse, which broke away and ran. Husband and wife were thrown from the buggy; Mrs. Johnson sustained a serious skull fracture. The creature, disappointed by the horse's escape, attacked her but was driven away by Mr. Johnson. The

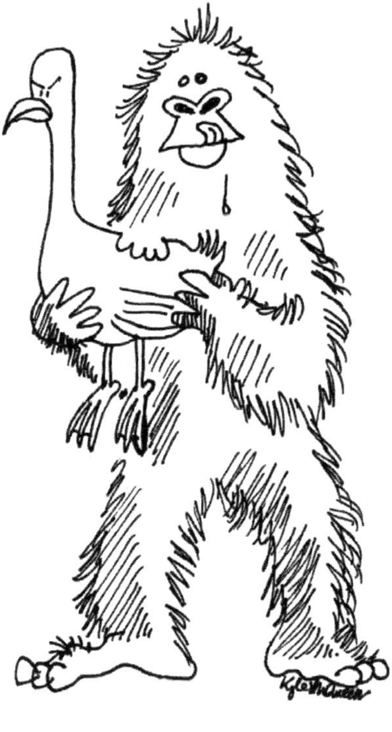

monster leaped a fence and disappeared in a cornfield. It was seen many times by residents but was too quick to be cornered or shot. Nobody could identify the creature, but the old standard explanation was trotted out: whatever it was, it must have escaped from a circus.

THE UNSEEN SPEAK

Mrs. Bob McLaughlin of Bloomfield had tuberculosis. In 1887, that was practically a death sentence, so she and her husband knew that the end was near. As his wife lay in her sickbed, Mr. McLaughlin often heard a disembodied feminine voice say, "Oh, Bob." He heard it at home; he heard it when running errands in town. When he walked to and from Bloomfield, the voice seemed to emanate from the roadside. It wasn't a hallucination because Mrs. McLaughlin heard it, too. In fact, she thought she recognized it as being the voice of Bob's first wife.

A wake was held when Mrs. McLaughlin passed away; the mourners consisted of a dozen friends, including a Reverend Foulk. That night, as everyone spoke in hushed whispers, they all heard a "strange, weird and unnatural" voice call out, "Oh, Bob!" The mourners peered into the coffin, thinking that perhaps Mrs. McLaughlin had only been in a coma and had revived, but she was dead beyond question. No one present could explain the phenomenon, which ceased forever when Mrs. McLaughlin was buried two days later.

At about the same time, Alexander Daugherty of Washington had a similar experience. One day in May 1887, he was resting in his Flora Street house when he heard footsteps of some invisible person approaching, followed by the voice of a woman repeating the phrase, "Brother Alex! Brother Alex!" He immediately recognized it as his sister's voice. A couple of days later, he received a telegram informing him that she had died at her home in Texas.

THE HAUNTED BENNETT HOUSE

In summer 1895, Nannie Bennett shocked Jeffersonville by poisoning herself and her two children, Omer and Lottie, with morphine. Mrs. Bennett had presumably gone insane from mourning her husband, Benson, who had paved the way for his family by swallowing poison in September 1893. She had planned every detail of the murder-suicide, including leaving three piles of burial clothes on a sofa and a note beginning with the words, "We are no more." By the time the bodies were found on July 1, they had been decomposing for three days.

A couple of years later, it was reported that no one was willing to live in the tragic house at 278 East Maple Street. Renters moved in and then quickly moved out, usually without a word of explanation. The few who would talk claimed that the place was haunted. A Mr. Eversole said that he had been disturbed by the sound of some invisible person walking downstairs. One night, he saw a white figure moving noiselessly from room to room. He found the unexpected guest so objectionable that he and his family spent the rest of the night in the yard. A newspaper account of the hauntings ends significantly: "Julius Louis, owner of the house, denounces the stories as arrant nonsense, but he refused to allow a reporter to stay in the house during the past night for purposes of investigation."

The Hard-Luck Cripe Family

Abraham Cripe, a German, lived with his family on a farm located three miles south of Rochester at the dusk of the nineteenth century and the dawn of the twentieth. Since the 1860s, it was said that the house occupied by the Cripes was haunted. Ghosts or no, enough dreadful deeds transpired there to result in the nickname "the House of Many Tragedies." An official scorecard of the calamities befalling the Cripes and related family members:

- Mrs. Cripe committed suicide by setting a haystack on fire in the barn and jumping into it.
- Only a few days later, Mr. Cripe and his sister dropped dead while working in the yard.
- A month later, son Lucien Cripe went insane after a limb fell on his head in the orchard.
- Loran Cripe was mysteriously murdered.
- Mr. Cripe's brother Elias was murdered in his barn the day after he sold some land. The crime was never solved.
- Elias Cripe's sons, Clark and Jay, went insane.
- Relative George Ford committed suicide.
- George Cripe was killed in an accident.

- In December 1904, Wilson Burns (Abraham's son-in-law) murdered his wife, Joseph Cripe and Aunt Margaret Braham and then committed suicide.

The house was at last torn down in January 1905, but even that did not put a stop to the hard luck. On September 9, family member Samuel Horn was killed while hauling logs. After that, only two family members remained. They must have considered legally changing their last name.

THE FACE AT THE WINDOW

Sophia Scharf died at her home at East Fifth and Spring Streets, New Albany, on December 2, 1891. Evidently, her spirit was not ready to move on to its reward because ten days later, her daughter-in-law, Mrs. Frank Zoeller, who lived at East Eighth and Sycamore Streets, saw the face of the late Mrs. Scharf staring through her window, a sight that took Mrs. Zoeller slightly aback. She called in witnesses, including Mrs. Peter Weinman, Fritz Weinman, two daughters of police officer Dennis Gleason and several others. The face eventually left but returned a second time that evening; on the return visit, the face was somehow imprinted in the pane of glass. Many persons rubbed the window in an attempt to remove it, but the image disappeared only when Joseph Scharf, the dead woman's son, passed a handkerchief over it. The significance of the act escaped comprehension, but it must have meant something.

MRS. FREEMAN'S FULL HOUSE

It is one thing when a believer in spirits sees a ghost. It is another when a skeptic sees one. Such was Mrs. Dell Freeman, who lived in a century-old house on First Street in Vincennes, in which a man was once murdered. In the years 1887 and 1888, she was plagued—mostly between the hours of 4:00 and 5:00 a.m.—by guitar music from an unseen musician, weird noises including the sound of "someone in fearful distress," doors that opened and closed themselves and, worst of all (or best of all, depending on one's point of view), full-bodied apparitions. One day, she saw a tall, slender man in her cellar who had no business being there. She sent a man downstairs to remonstrate with the otherworldly stranger. He followed the figure and watched it for some time until it vanished "like a puff of smoke." On another occasion, a ghostly man stepped out from behind a bookcase and glared at people assembled in the room. It disappeared when approached. Once, everyone in the house saw a blue flame sweep down from the ceiling. "The clock there took a spell one night," said Mrs. Freeman, "and played 'Home, Sweet Home' and 'In the Sweet By and By.' Others heard it besides myself."

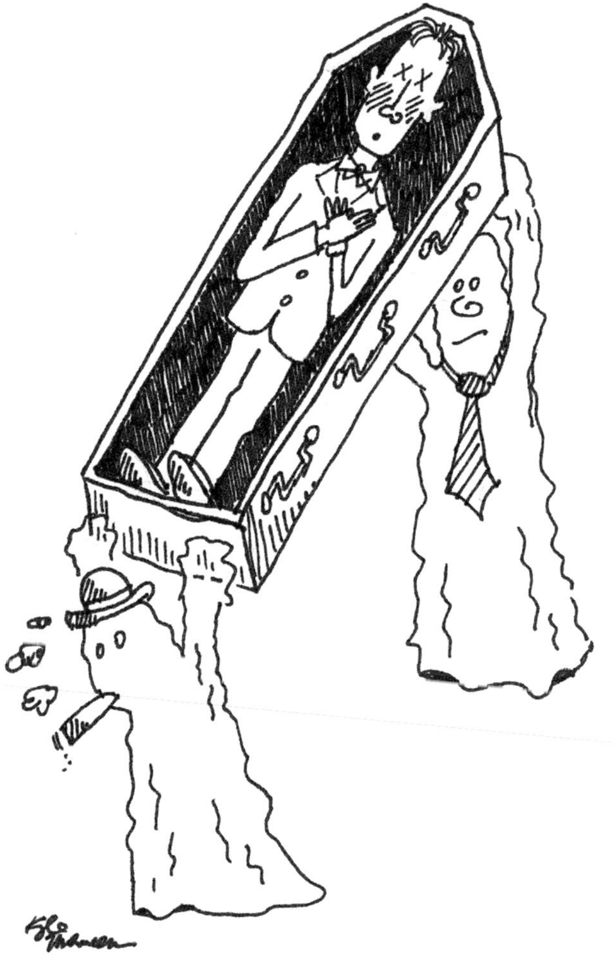

(One assumes it was not supposed to do that.) The most improbable manifestation of all came one night when Mrs. Freeman saw two ghosts with "hideous shapes" carrying a black velvet lidless coffin through a room: "In the coffin could be plainly seen a dark-faced man." Mrs. Freeman, who took no stock in spooks, specters or Spiritualists, believed that a magician was somehow entering her house and performing tricks to convince her to move out for some nefarious reason. She took comfort in this explanation.

A GLIDING GHOST

In January 1884, six men lost their lives in a train wreck near Broad Ripple, eight miles north of Indianapolis. Not surprisingly, the spot was afterward declared haunted. Reports of ghosts were vague and murky until four years later, when people began seeing a ghostly woman who glided along the tracks to the river's edge. Once there, she would walk on the water right up to the Louisville, New Albany and Chicago Railroad Bridge. She was spotted at least three times, including the night of February 23, 1888; witnesses included "some of the most worthy people in the village," according to one account.

Another spirit with an affinity for trains loitered at the Franklin depot in fall 1889. A conductor on the Jeffersonville, Madison and Indianapolis Railroad first saw it on the night of October 28 as it meandered up and down the depot platform. After that, it was seen many times by many citizens, including two boys named Hill and Jackson, who swore that it chased them from the depot platform until it vanished. The best description they could give was that it resembled "a man walking in a stooping position and dressed in full white." Edward Pierce shot the ghost several times one night; "at every shot [it] would utter a piteous whine," but the bullets seemed to have no effect and the thing disappeared before Pierce's eyes. Citizens had two conflicting theories about the ghost's presence: 1) the depot had been built on an old cemetery and perhaps the ghost was the remnant of a person who was expressing his displeasure because his body had not been properly removed; 2) the ghost was actually J.M. Dunlap, proprietor of a nearby coal yard, attempting to scare would-be thieves away from his precious lumps. It may be significant that the spirit failed to make an appearance after its fame had spread sufficiently to attract a large crowd of onlookers.

A Haunted Hoosegow

On September 4, 1885, Marshal John Cole of Jeffersonville arrested Tim Sullivan for public intoxication. As Sullivan was an Irishman, his drunkenness surprised absolutely no one. However, Sullivan did startle Cole a couple of days later when he fulfilled a promise to commit suicide by hanging himself from a brace in cell number two. Soon after Sullivan joined his ancestors in the mystic land of Tír na nÓg, Marshal Cole noticed that inexplicable noises occasionally emanated from cell number two, but he paid them no mind—until October 1886, that is. Cole was working late; no one else was in the jailhouse. Suddenly, he heard the sound of a body swinging to and fro from the gratings, accompanied by choking noises. The nervous lawman investigated and found nothing that could account for what he heard except a broken piece of guttering, which he had repaired without delay. That night, Cole heard the sounds again. After that, the dreadful noises came frequently and at all hours of the day and night. In August 1889, a poor woman with a child received permission to spend a night in the jail, as she had nowhere else to go. About midnight, she came charging out of the cell, claiming that a man had been "after her." The officers demonstrated to her satisfaction that she had been the only person in the jailhouse that night, but she took leave of them to find some more congenial shelter.

"I am not a believer in ghosts, nor am I superstitious, but that there is some strange being about the jail I am certain," the marshal told a *Louisville Courier-Journal* correspondent in August 1889. Two other officers told the journalist that they also had heard the noises. Indeed, every person who had worked at the jail since September 1885 had witnessed the sounds; some observed that the noises got louder as the anniversary of Sullivan's suicide approached. Naturally, the reporter could not resist investigating; on the night of

August 31, he—accompanied by a half dozen intrepid souls—went to the Jeffersonville jail. Not being fools, some of the investigators stayed inside and some stayed outside, in order to rule out trickery or collusion. The reporter and his friends inspected the building until they were certain that no one else was hiding there. He thus described the night's festivities:

> *Within ten minutes after the investigators arrived, the noise commenced and was such that those who heard it are not anxious to listen to it again. At first it sounded as if some heavy object was swinging against the iron doors in a struggle. It became next a gurgling, as if someone was strangling, and this was followed by a low cough. Another beating against the bars and all was quiet. How many times this was repeated is not known, as those who had listened once were satisfied and went away.*

Tales from the Tombs

Death, Be Not Boring

Most of us live ordinary lives and die ordinary deaths, such as by having a heart attack or choking on a cheeseburger. Some people, however, dare to expire in creative ways that surprise the bystander and delight the newspaper editor. Here are the stories of several Hoosiers who did exactly that.

Perhaps James A. Moore should have been an engineer or an inventor, as he clearly was skillful at building clever devices. Instead, Moore was a farmer—and a suicidal one at that. He lived with his wife and three children about fifteen miles south of Lafayette. On the night of June 10, 1876, he traveled to the Lahr House in the big city, paying for his room a few days in advance and saying that he wanted to work on an invention during his stay. After checking in, Moore paid a visit to Harding and Sons' machine shop, where he had the proprietors rivet a couple of fourteen-inch iron bars to the head of a sharp broadaxe. Then he had two eight-foot pieces of wood attached to the iron bars. He carried all these things back to his room, along with a shorter piece of wood, a box, some chloroform, a cord, a candle, some straps and a large wad of cotton. If the hotel staff saw him dragging this strange equipment into their establishment and wondered what he was up to, they would soon have their curiosity satisfied.

Once alone in his room, Moore stood the two long pieces of wood upright and secured them, side by side, to the floor with hinges. He joined a smaller plank between the two long pieces so that it made a crossbar. He raised the axe to the top of his structure, point facing downward, and held it in place with a cord attached to the wall. Moore arranged the box so that the axe blade would hit it if it fell. If the reader has not already guessed, Moore had fashioned a homemade guillotine. When he decided the time was right, he placed the lit candle so that it would eventually burn the cord holding the axe in two. Then he strapped himself to the floor and placed his head on the box, which contained the wad of cotton soaked in chloroform. As he breathed the fumes, he went unconscious—presumably—just before the cord burned in half and the heavy axe blade fell. The axe weighed fifty pounds and dropped about fifteen feet. When hotel staff came to investigate, they found Moore utterly beheaded. The axe had landed with such force that it was embedded in the floorboards. Doubtless, Moore's widow was aggrieved at her loss but relieved that he decided to

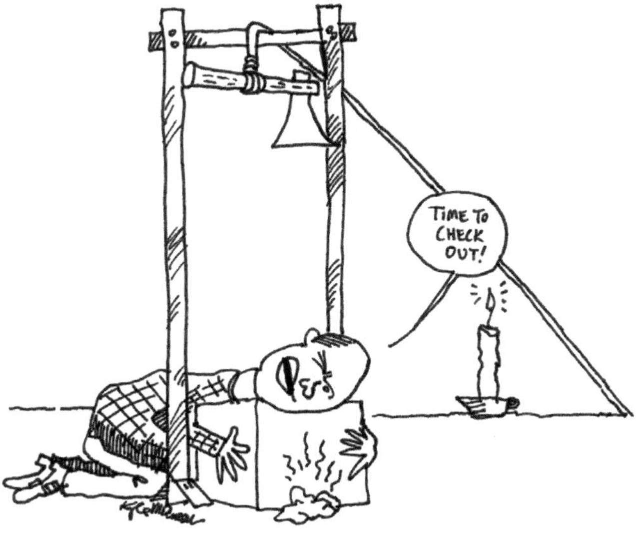

pull off this science experiment in a hotel room rather than in her parlor.

In *My Life and Hard Times*, humorist James Thurber writes that one of his relatives was a tree surgeon who died of chestnut blight. Thurber's joke had a real-life counterpart in James Hair, a hostler of New Albany. After ministering to a sick horse in April 1879, Hair contracted a fatal case of the glanders, a disease common in horses and mules but virtually unheard of in humans. In case you ever have occasion to wonder if you have contracted the glanders, these are the symptoms that appear in the human body: swelling of the face, throat and feet; prodigiously runny nose; high fever; discolored face; exhaustion; great difficulty eating.

Asahel ("Ace") Kelly of Winchester had a reputation for being something of an adventurer and world traveler. Eventually, he returned home and settled down to life as a restaurateur. This mode of life evidently was not to his liking, and he overdosed on morphine in a Cincinnati hotel room on May 13, 1893, at age thirty-two. His death was remarkable for the facetious tone of his suicide note, which read in part:

> *You can do as you please about burying me, but don't plant me at Winchester. If you can't take me to Montezuma give me to some doctor…You will find me a rusty looking corpse, as I have not shaved for two weeks nor bathed for a month. Don't have any religious exercises over me, whatever you do. By way of amusement you might have somebody whistle "Johnny Comes Marching Home," and if any of our pious relatives want to shed tears, kindly fire a few rocks at them. Don't you open the box or coffin, or whatever I am in, as I don't want those hypocrites to have the satisfaction of seeing me dead.*

Andrew Cain and William Grosc went coon hunting near Montpelier on October 3, 1895. Finding it a chilly night, they built a campfire, unaware that someone had buried a cache of nitroglycerin on the very spot. They never had a chance to find it out: nearby trees were decorated with bits and pieces of the hunters in the milliseconds before being pulled up by the roots.

Boys will be boys—and one thing boys loved to do in the days before television sapped all their anarchistic creativity was to recreate the legend of William Tell. Judging from old newspaper accounts, it seldom ended well. For example, on March 14, 1896, two thirteen-year-olds named Albert Isaacs and Elmer Ross played William Tell at Evansville. Ross put something on his head—the papers don't say whether it was the canonical apple—while Isaacs tried to shoot it off with a Flobert rifle. His aim was off just a little, but that was sufficient.

In his 1984 book *The Choking Doberman*, folklorist Jan Harold Brunvand discusses the origins of the earwig urban legend. Perhaps the reader has not heard the earwig urban legend? The story goes that the insect crawls into someone's ear and slowly burrows its way through the brain until it finally emerges at the opposite ear, where a doctor extracts it—but the earwig laid eggs en route and soon the poor sufferer has a brain *full* of earwigs! As it turns out, something like this actually happened. On February 14, 1897, Mrs. William Swan of Elkhart was dying of a larvae infestation in her head. The previous summer, an unspecified type of bug had lodged in her ear and doctors were unable to remove it. Evidently, the insect had been pregnant. The report ends: "Mrs. Swan became deranged with pain, but will soon be relieved by death." Incidentally, Happy Valentine's Day!

John Kelley, a wealthy farmer who lived near Woodland, had escaped twice from the Logansport Insane Hospital. The big-hearted authorities finally chose to let the maniac stay at home with his wife and children. On December 14, 1897, he went to the barn and lit a stick of dynamite with a long fuse. As the fuse slowly burned down, Kelley hanged himself from a rafter. In the following explosion, Kelley's arms and legs were blown off, his clothing was set afire and fragments of both barn and Kelley came raining down, all of which provides insight into why he was sent to the asylum in the first place.

On September 20, 1901, two ten-year-old Winchester boys, Omer Pelee and Emil Miller, played a little game in which they reenacted the recent assassination of President McKinley—using a real rifle as a prop. Miller played Czolgosz, the assassin, while Pelee played McKinley. The coroner played himself.

Another Indiana child who might have met her maker by means of reckless playing was May Levcsay of Jeffersonville, who jumped rope 160 times without a break in March 1902. Several days later, she developed a painful abscess in her stomach, which the doctor theorized had been caused by her rope-jumping feat. Her case ended fatally on April 23.

Thomas Foley, a drunk and abusive husband, sued his wife for divorce in the town of English in April 1902. She had attempted to murder him by coating his hands, face and clothing with salt while he was drunk, tying his hands and feet and leaving him out in the field in the fond hope that the cows would "lick him to death." Foley did not die—he suffered nothing worse than raw skin and shredded clothing—but his wife's creativity must be acknowledged.

A ghastly accident almost beyond comprehension occurred at the Grand Hotel in Indianapolis on August 24, 1902. "The elevator has two entrances, the rear door having been left open," explained a news article. Occupant Luke Ryan leaned back and was instantly crushed with so much force that his body was forced entirely through a hole only five inches wide.

In March 1903, Martin Myers of Logansport cut a tree in such a manner that it would fall on a nearby stump. He then knelt with his head on the stump and waited for a strong gust of wind to send the tree falling. When it finally happened, Myers's skull was pulverized, and he became probably the only person ever to commit suicide by means of a falling tree.

Had Myers not given in to the self-destructive urge, he could have attended the carnival that came to Logansport three months after his death. There he would have seen one of the featured attractions, a performer who ate live snakes. Twelve-year-old Alice Fairchild (a lovely name, that!) was so inspired by the act that it fired within her soul the burning urge to imitate the circus geek. Her obliging brother caught a dozen snakes, which little Alice tried to consume. The serpents did not desire to be eaten alive, and bit her before she could bite them.

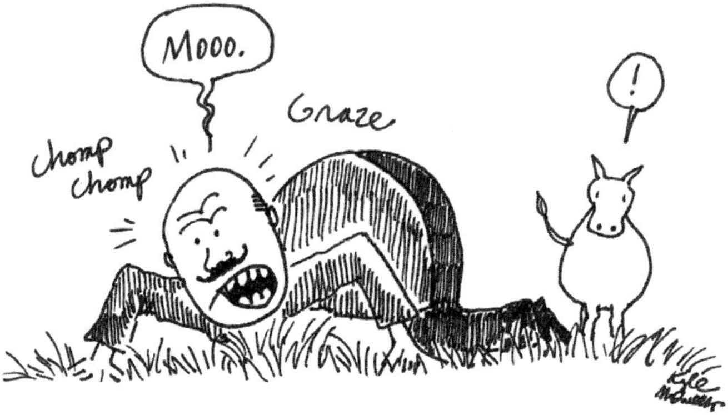

Kokomo doctor Edward Stanton, formerly wealthy but in later years a pauper, had been insane for years. He labored under the delusion that he was an ox; often, he ate grass in the field along with the herd of cattle at the county poor farm. When he died at age eighty in June 1903, an autopsy revealed that his mouth and stomach were full of grass. Verdict: Stanton had accidentally eaten some poisonous herb along with his usual fare.

Wilbur Todd was the leading man in the Windfall Comedy Company, an acting troupe that happened to be playing in a production ironically titled *Blood-and-Thunder* at the Gas City Opera House in Marion on December 19, 1903. He felt a trifle suicidal that night and so placed a live round in a prop revolver. After announcing, "It's me to the hot place," Todd placed the gun to his head and pulled the trigger. The audience received their money's worth that night.

William Marsh died at his home in Henderson, Kentucky, in early March 1904. Afterward, his family got a telegram informing them that by some mysterious dispensation of Providence, Marsh's twin brother had died at the same hour on the same day in Marion, Indiana.

Charles E. Bliss of Peru was a man of his word. He moved to Sedalia, Missouri, in 1904, where he fell in love with a woman called "Ten" Moore. On the night of September 19, Bliss proposed playing a game of cards with Moore. "What will we play for?" she asked. Bliss answered, "I will stake my life against yours." Mrs. Moore won the game, and Bliss proved that he was a good sport by committing suicide on the spot.

Mysteries abounded when Charles Howard's body was found at South Bend on September 25, 1905. His corpse was standing upright in a lake in Notre Dame Cemetery (aka Cedar Lake Cemetery), with his head just above the waterline; he was wearing a hat and leaning on a cane, as though he had been casually standing on a street corner. Strangest of all, he was a lifelong invalid, so how did he get there in the first place?

William Lieberenz of Stroh got angry at his wife on July 14, 1905, and took a shot at her. She got away, and Lieberenz realized that she would return with the cops. He made up his mind to kill himself before the authorities arrived. To achieve this agreeable purpose, he drank some wood alcohol. When this proved ineffective, he ate a quantity of Paris Green, a popular insecticide. Result: nothing. The impatient Lieberenz grabbed a razor and slit both his wrists. The Death Angel still proved coy, so the beleaguered gentleman shot himself in the head. Still no luck. At last, he crawled to a cabinet, found a razor and cut his own throat, leaving behind a puzzle for the coroner and a mess for his widow to clean up.

While making a business trip to Sylvester, Georgia, in December 1906, wealthy T. Kirby Heinsohn of Muncie had a dream in which he was shaving himself. He awoke to find a razor in his hand and his throat cut. He survived just long enough to write an explanation.

Was Mrs. James Daly killed by her illness or the power of suggestion? The Evansville housewife had been sick for several days when she found herself the subject of an erroneous obituary in a local paper. The death notice troubled her so greatly that she suffered a relapse. The incorrect report became true on April 8, 1907.

The wives of Zack Watson of New Harmony seemed to have uniquely hard luck. The first Mrs. Watson took sick after cleaning the parlor and died in March 1905. The second Mrs. Watson also took sick after cleaning the parlor and died in March 1906. The third Mrs. Watson—well, you get the drift. She died in March 1907. All three women had similar symptoms; it was thought at first that they had each died of spinal meningitis. Then someone realized that March is spring cleaning time. The fatal parlor was examined, and investigators found that the old wallpaper was coated with a recently outlawed poisonous substance. Each Mrs. Watson had breathed particles of the poison after brushing down the parlor walls with a broom. The grieving widower promised that he would replace the wallpaper as soon as possible.

Joseph B. Hamilton, a farmer who lived east of Salem, killed himself with a shotgun on June 28, 1909. Before doing so, however, he had thoughtfully saved someone some trouble by digging his own grave in the family burying ground.

Lloyd Magon, a seventeen-year-old poetry buff in Hammond, found the mystical elements in the work of Edgar Allan Poe difficult to understand. So difficult, in fact, that he shot himself out of sheer frustration on January 7, 1911.

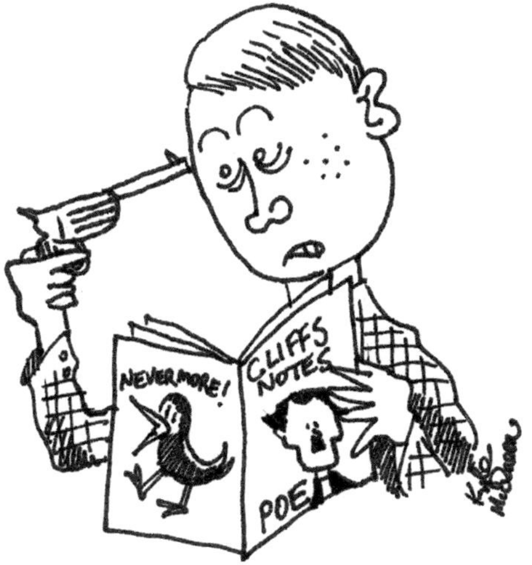

An Oakland City barber named Forest Butler, disappointed in love—for barbers need love, too—partook of strychnine in his shop just before Valentine's Day 1911. Soon afterward, a customer entered, and Butler, finding it worthwhile to collect one final nickel, gave his patron such an inadequate shave that the latter complained. "If you had taken what I have you would be nervous, too," said the barber, who expired minutes later.

James Bixler of New Albany was a vengeful suicide. He took himself off by drinking a bottle of carbolic acid in front of his recently divorced wife's house on February 8, 1909, which spoiled her night. He left a note in which he stated that he wanted his body to be buried on the riverbank in such a location that his former wife would have to pass his grave every time she went to draw water.

Another suicide with attitude was Margaret Gann, who drowned herself in a pond near Evansville on June 7, 1911. A news account tells us the aftermath: "She left a note stating she hoped her husband, who had abandoned her, could be permitted to gaze upon her dead face. The husband was found and the last wish of the dead wife was gratified."

A SMORGASBORD OF SKELETONS

In May 1860, the town of Vevay was hit by a storm that blew down a large sycamore, leaving behind a hollow stump about eight feet high. To make the scene even more picturesque, the stump stood upright in Indian Creek. There it forlornly rested for seventeen years. In December 1877, Simon Cusart set fire to the stump and noticed a disagreeable odor emanating from it. Upon inspection, Cusart found a human skeleton within, along with a wool sock and some buttons. It was assumed that the skeleton was the mortal remains of John C. Cline, a German immigrant who was the neighborhood's only missing person. Cline had boarded for fourteen years with the family of William Tilley, a farmer who lived just a few hundred yards from the tree. The missing man had left the Tilley house in 1871, saying that he was going to Philadelphia to get money and would be back soon. He never returned, and the best anyone could figure was that while still close to home Cline had been murdered and stuffed into the hollow tree.

A similar case turned up near Montpelier in February 1888. Two woodcutters chopped down a tree and found a skeleton nestled inside. He was probably Van Richardson, a shoemaker who had vanished about 1878. The only hole in the tree was a small one about ten feet from the ground, so some enterprising murderer who was not afraid of a little hard work must have cut the body into fragments and stuffed them, one by one, through the hole in the tree by means of a ladder.

James Shackleford was walking on the shore of the Ohio River near Alton on May 6, 1901, minding his own business, when he noticed a partially buried skeleton. Shackleford commenced digging and soon unearthed complete remains. The most interesting feature was that the skeleton was wearing old-fashioned, rusty handcuffs. No one knew the identity of the unfortunate, but a local legend fit the bill quite nicely. It was remembered that about a quarter century before, two men were arrested for thievery in Brandenburg, Kentucky, and were sentenced to five years in prison. One of the convicts was a physical giant, surly, sadistic and full of gratuitous cruelty. He was so strong that he could break any set of handcuffs the sheriff put on him. Officers loaded the prisoners on a boat and rode down the Ohio en route to the prison at Frankfort, Kentucky. When the boat neared Alton during the night, the strong prisoner picked up his handcuffed partner in crime and threw him overboard, apparently just for the meanness of it. When the manacled skeleton was found in 1901, it was theorized that the drowned prisoner had been found at last.

Readers of my book *Forgotten Tales of Kentucky* will recall the plethora of giant human skeletons that have been found in the Bluegrass State over the years. It appears that prehistoric Goliaths settled in Indiana as well. In 1879, the state archaeologist supervised the excavation of a stone mound located on the Brewersville property of a man named Robinson. Scientists found a number of skeletons, including that of a whopper who measured nine feet, eight inches in life. The giant wore a mica necklace, and weapons found nearby were "unlike those used by the Indians." The

Robinson family kept the skeleton, perhaps as a conversation piece. It was lost in a flood in 1937. In November 1902, a man working on Andrew Keesling's farm near Cadiz pried up a tree stump he had just blasted and found a giant skeleton underneath. The rings on the stump indicated that the tree had been growing atop the bones for at least two hundred years. The news report of this incident noted, "On various occasions several gigantic skeletons have been found in a gravel pit on the same farm." The very next month, a prehistoric graveyard was found in a mound on Solomon Hedrick's farm near LaGrange. Hedrick had owned the farm for several years before he finally decided to excavate the mound, which was thirty feet high, covered four acres and "resembled a loaf of bread" in shape. It was made of gravel and sand, which its builders must have imported from some distance away since there was no gravel or sand on the surrounding land. They had even constructed a roadway twenty feet in height leading to the top of the mound. Twelve feet below the surface, Hedrick found a number of skeletons of humans who had been eight feet in height or more. Their teeth were in notably good shape. In addition to the remains of giants, Hedrick also found a wealth of trinkets, ivory beads and a shield made of bone. In 1925, a mound at Walkerton yielded eight giant skeletons clad in copper armor; the runts of the litter were eight feet long, while the big boys measured nine feet in length.

While digging a trench in the basement of St. Francis Xavier's Cathedral in Vincennes in October 1901,

Thomas Richardville found the skeletons of two children and an adult. It was estimated that the bodies had been there at least two hundred years and probably were all that was mortal of French pioneers. It was thought that they had been placed in a burying ground, and years later, the church was inadvertently built on top of them. One newspaper couldn't resist noting that "[o]ne of the skeletons was almost perfect, even to the hair, which lay parted on the skull, and was a dark red color. The hair fell off and crumbled when the skeleton was lifted." The remains were reburied in a nearby Catholic cemetery despite the best efforts of relic hunters, who wanted to carry away the bones for who knows what purposes.

During the Civil War, a trapper named Steele dwelt on an island in the Kankakee River near Richmond. In 1861, the neighbors cast a disapproving eye on Steele when an overnight guest, a government agent named Barrington, disappeared. Barrington's horse was found wandering in the woods the next day, but there was no trace of either the agent or the $10,000 in government money he was known to have had on his person. Local opinion of Steele became even more scathing later in the same year, when his wife and daughter also vanished from human sight. Steele was threatened with lynching. He took the hint and disappeared, never to be seen again. Steele's house was left abandoned to the elements, as no one particularly cared to live there. On July 20, 1905, workers tearing down the house found five skeletons behind a cellar wall: three males and two females.

Speculation held that the remains of Barrington, Mrs. Steele and Steele's daughter had been discovered, along with two hitherto unsuspected victims as a bonus.

LIBELING THE DEAD

George Salada died at Bedford in February 1901, after which his mother Cleopatra hired photographer Newton Erins to snap a memorial photo of the corpse, a common practice at the time. Mrs. Salada was unhappy with the photo—perhaps Erins failed to get George's good side—and refused to pay for it. The miffed photographer got even in April by posting the photo of George's body in a public place with the phrase "Dead Beat" scrawled on it. Mrs. Salada did not appreciate Erins's witty pun and sued him for libel.

If we wish to be technical, what Reverend Clarence Miller did was slander rather than libel, but the effect was the same as in the Salada case: vastly displeased next of kin. On July 14, 1901, Miller delivered the following eulogy at the funeral of Congressman A.N. Martin at Bluffton: "It would have been better if Mr. Martin would have been shot on the field of battle than to have lived to lead the life he did. He was in public office the better portion of his life, and made in one office $100,000, but was sent home for burial in a cheap pine coffin, furnished by the government. His life has been a tragedy, and the use of liquor made it so."

Another preacher who got into hot water by being too honest was Reverend Mr. Balgan, who officiated at the funeral of coal miner Charles Robbins at Ellsworth on January 30, 1906. "Hell was made for just such men," was one of the more memorable statements made during the obsequies. The miners in attendance protested that even though Robbins had lived a life of sin, it was not sporting to criticize him at his own funeral. Then they hoisted the coffin and carried it to the cemetery, a half mile away, and performed their own crude but heartfelt ceremony at Robbins's grave.

THE VENGEFUL EPITAPH

In the mid-1870s, an unnamed elderly lady of Adams County deeded her farm to her son-in-law, who promised he would take care of her as long as she lived. Instead, less than a year later, he kicked her out and she had to move into the county poorhouse. There she died on June 17, 1878. Her son was too young at the time to help her, but he got sweet revenge a couple of decades later when, in 1901, he had a monument erected on her grave that bore an epitaph immortalizing the son-in-law's villainy:

Robbed of all her earthly possessions
By one who made such great professions;
He's worse than a rascal, thief, or knave.
He sent my poor mother to a pauper's grave.

In that grand morn when the trumpet shall sound,
My mother will rise from this pauper grave;
Her robes shall be white, without spot or shade;
But where is C.S.? Not far from Hades.

YOU CAN TAKE IT WITH YOU

South Jenkins, a Posey County pioneer, died at Mount Vernon at age seventy-nine on March 3, 1903. At his request, he was buried with a shotgun, a powder horn and a razor.

A similar, but far more tragic, incident occurred when seven-year-old Dorothy Fountain died at Wabash in April 1903. She had contracted a long illness, and when she realized that recovery was impossible, she asked that she be buried with her favorite doll. The doll and her owner were dressed in matching outfits when placed in the casket.

In November 1902, Hattie Larkin of Marion had a lover's quarrel with her boyfriend, William Gallapo. He demanded that she return his photograph. She refused, saying that she had a place for it. The place she had in mind became evident when the eighteen-year-old committed suicide by taking morphine and requested that she be buried holding the photo.

When William Selzer died in Evansville in September 1914, he was buried at his own request with two cigars of his favorite brand in his vest pocket.

FUNERAL SPOILERS

Premature burial was a common fate in the days when comas were not fully understood and primitive methods were used to tell whether life was extinct. Here are the stories of several Indiana residents who had hairbreadth escapes from being cast into a living grave.

Elderly Eliza Weir of Memphis, Clark County, was being laid out for burial one June day in 1879—with good cause, for she had just died after a long bout with rheumatism. She had no pulse and her skin was cold, so the undertaker thought she was good to go. Bodies were buried quickly during hot weather in those pre-embalming days, so within fifty minutes of Mrs. Weir's demise the mortician had placed coins on her eyes, bound her jaw with a strip of cloth and fulfilled all the other funerary necessities. The neighbors came in to view the body. Suddenly, the would-be corpse sat up and made some unintelligible remarks, much to the consternation of the mourners. She soon returned to full consciousness. Had she awakened only a little while later, she would have found herself in very unpleasant circumstances.

D.A. Pangburn of Oregon Township, near Charlestown, had the unenviable experience of dying twice in the same week. On August 6, 1885, he passed away from pneumonia. He was "laid out for the grave"—but, fortunately for him, not embalmed—and attendants were surprised to hear him suddenly ask for a drink of water. He rallied briefly and then died for the second time that night. Pangburn's brother arrived on August 7, just in time to see the dead man arise again. "During the whole time," wrote a reporter, "he was dimly conscious of all that passed around him, but was powerless to move or speak."

About 1892, the Reverend E.R. Johnson of Mulberry died of typhoid—sort of. The undertaker prepared the body for burial; friends held a two-day wake. The funeral sermon was preached. The choir was singing the closing hymn. And then Reverend Johnson ruined everything by sitting up in his casket! The effect this had on the mourners need not be gone into. Johnson was unable to speak for three days, but then regained his health and lived another decade. He died for good—we think—on September 28, 1902.

Emma Taylor had a particularly disturbing close brush with premature burial, although the experience surely cannot be considered much fun even under the best conditions. She died on January 12, 1901, in Brazil, Indiana, and was fully dressed and prepared for burial when she suddenly revived before onlookers. A newspaper report stated that she was cognizant of the horrid fate that almost befell her: "She was conscious some minutes before she recovered strength to move and could hear and understand the cries of the mourners and kind words uttered over her supposed lifeless form by sorrowing friends."

Mrs. Charles Edwards's week-old baby died in Jeffersonville on November 10, 1902; "several reputable physicians" agreed on that. Yet, as undertaker George Shrader crossed the threshold of his establishment with his newest charge, the child started crying. It seemed to be just fine after that.

Joseph Barker died in Evansville in February 1903. Imagine the shock that undertaker Schaefer received when Barker sat up just as he was about to be embalmed!

Michael Hoetzel, an elderly German, collapsed in his Jeffersonville home on May 22, 1905. His sons called in a doctor, who pronounced the old man dead. The undertaker came and had started making arrangements when the "corpse" yawned, stretched and requested a glass of beer.

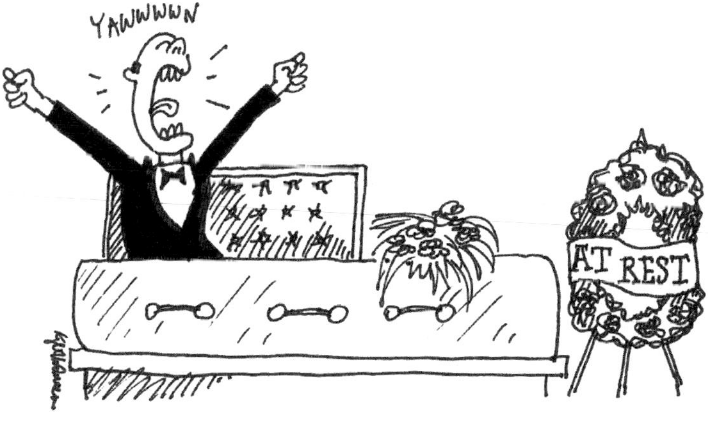

The aforementioned people on this list are the lucky ones who barely escaped waking up in an enclosed box under six feet of earth. There were also occasions on which souls *might* have been buried alive, but nobody can say for sure. For example, Joseph Hutchins of Boswell was subject to falling into trances. He had been pronounced dead twice in his lifetime only to recover before he was consigned to the earth. He died for a third time on February 28, 1886, and was buried. But rumors spread that he had been alive when inhumed, and thirty-six hours later he was exhumed. Despite having spent so long underground—and in winter, yet—Hutchins was "warm around the heart." Nevertheless, he was reburied, only to be dug up a second time by nervous neighbors. Was Hutchins buried prematurely? The mystery remains.

Nat Chandler died of exposure to the elements at Alfordsville and was buried on November 19, 1894. A doctor thought that Chandler might be in a state of suspended animation due to the cold but chose to say nothing about it. A month later, the physician mentioned his theory to someone—nice of him to bring it up eventually—and soon rumors were spreading that Chandler had been buried alive. It was remembered that his body had been warm "although it had lain on the frozen ground for several hours," that his arms and legs had been flexible and that "there was no appearance of death in the face." In addition, a barber who had shaved the alleged corpse had accidentally nicked its ear, and blood flowed freely as it would if Chandler's heart were beating. When the authorities asked Chandler's family if they wanted his body exhumed, they refused on the grounds that they might be better off not knowing the truth.

John S. Briggs, president of the New Albany Light, Heat and Power Company, died of heart failure on January 20, 1895. Or maybe he didn't. Years before, Briggs had made a pact with his wife that whoever survived the other would put off embalming and burial until it was certain the deceased was deceased—such was their fear of premature burial. A newspaper account relates that more than three days after Briggs's death, his un-embalmed body, which had

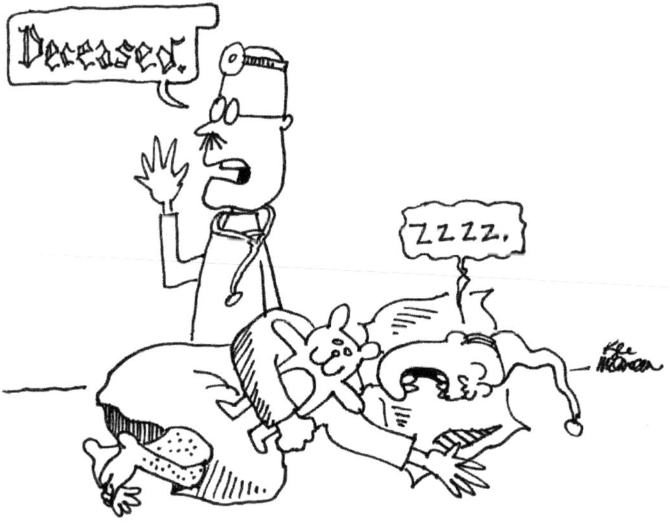

been left "in the sumptuously furnished parlor of the dead man's handsome residence," was unspoiled and fresh as a daisy. His complexion was pink and his cheeks unsunken. The doctor in attendance didn't want to talk to reporters about it, but declared that nothing unusual was going on. Briggs was buried at last on January 24; his family denied that previous reports about his uncanny lifelike appearance were true.

Susan Sulzer of Cannelton died as she entered her home on March 11, 1905. Two days later, her body was coffined and placed in a cemetery vault in preparation for burial. But whether she was truly dead was a matter of conjecture. Sharp-eyed persons noticed that a wound on her head continued to bleed and her face maintained a rosy shade. A doctor who pricked her finger drew blood, and no signs of decomposition set in. As late as eleven days after Sulzer's putative death, the question was unanswered.

On the other hand, apparent signs of life could be deceiving. Peter Biesen of Madison was buried on Sunday, March 10, 1889, after receiving injuries in a caving sand bank, despite the fact that the corpse remained warm. His friends, who stood watch over his grave, became increasingly worried that a mistake had been made. On Monday afternoon, they called in physicians, who examined the body after it was brought to the surface. They declared that despite Biesen's disturbingly lifelike appearance when buried, he had indeed been dead all along.

Then there were the people who were really and truly buried alive, such as Peter Trautman, a Bartholomew County pioneer. He died in 1836 and rested in peace—or so it seemed to blissfully ignorant surface dwellers—until May 22, 1895, when his remains were exhumed for reinterment elsewhere. The position of Trautman's skeleton revealed that he had turned over in his coffin.

Advance Warning

Walter Bower, a railroad brakeman of New Albany, had been troubled by a series of vividly detailed dreams that always climaxed with his falling off a train: "He would see the cars moving along at a rapid rate," a newspaper article recounted. "Everything would seem as bright as day. He could hear the clicking of the wheels, the whistle and engine bell. Then, while climbing along the side of a car he felt the handle give way and he dropped to the ground with one hand across the rail. He saw the picture of himself bleeding and unable to move while the train moved by." Bower was so disturbed by this recurring dream that he asked for a leave of absence from his job. But fate was not to be denied: in late June 1901, shortly after he came back to work, he fell off a train in the same manner detailed in his dream. Bower was taken to Louisville Hospital, where he begged doctors not to amputate his injured arm. By the time doctors decided that they had better break out the bonesaw, blood poisoning had set in, and Bower died of the injuries prophesied in his dreams.

Twice in the last week of September 1901, William Vickery of Gibson County dreamed that he would die in his mill on September 29. And yet he went to work as usual that day. He was found deceased in his mill in the afternoon.

Presumably for lack of a better topic, on July 24, 1905, Martin Conroy told his mother over breakfast that he had dreamed of getting killed while at his job on the Big Four Railroad. She begged him to stay at home that day, but he insisted on going. He was run over by a work train within seconds of stepping out of his Lawrenceburg house.

On the morning of April 23, 1910, Mrs. William Kuhlman of Evansville awoke from a dream in which she had heard her son Willie calling for her. She later found that at the same time she had had her nightmare, Willie had been killed in an accident at the Evansville and Terre Haute Railroad yard.

In September 1912, Mrs. William S. Slate of Indianapolis sent a creepy letter to Reverend Dr. H.C. Clippinger, pastor of Trinity Methodist Episcopal Church in New Albany, in which she informed him that she had an unshakable feeling that she would be dead within a year. She requested that the reverend preach at her funeral. Dr. Clippinger dismissed Mrs. Slate's worries on the grounds that she was only thirty-six years old and in excellent health. In March 1913, however, the prediction she had made six months earlier came true. Dr. Clippinger traveled to Indianapolis to keep his promise.

PECULIAR MANIFESTATIONS OF GRIEF

When Mrs. James Pound died in 1887, her husband made a solemn vow that he would never set foot in their house again, despite its choice location on the highway, two miles from New Washington. He kept his word. He and his children moved in with a sister-in-law, and no one ever entered the locked house. By 1902, the place had taken on a colorfully dilapidated appearance, as described in a contemporary news article:

> *Lace curtains hang in the windows, but it is said that the beds are unmade, the floors unswept and dishes are said to stand on the table with moldering food in them. The yard is overgrown with weeds, and an old ax rests on a woodpile in front of the house. Year after year Pound has plowed around the fence that surrounds the house, losing the use of more than an acre of ground.*

Pound would neither make repairs to the abandoned house nor allow anyone to rent it, and he watched closely to make sure that curious vandals did not enter.

In the late 1870s, Daniel Comstock was engaged in the construction of the Frankfort and Kokomo Railroad. He fell in love with eighteen-year-old Sallie May Byers of Frankfort. They became engaged and looked forward to a happy life together. But it was never to be; Miss Byers took ill and died before the wedding date. Comstock, brokenhearted, eventually left Frankfort when the railroad business dictated that he move elsewhere. He never married and no other woman ever took the place of his fiancée in his heart. In 1910, Comstock, by then very wealthy and living in New York, heard the news that the old cemetery in which Sallie May Byers was buried was about to be abandoned. The bodies were to be exhumed and moved elsewhere. After ascertaining that all of Sallie's relatives were dead, he hurried to Frankfort on a mission to claim her remains. He bought a plot in a new cemetery and had Sallie's casket unearthed and moved to her new resting grounds. Then he returned to his home in New York.

The cemetery at Charlestown was the scene of a mystery that puzzled locals for years. One morning, the caretaker, Elias Naudaine, found a brand-new, unauthorized grave without a marker. Because it was a small mound, everyone assumed it to be a child's grave. Hundreds of people visited the site, but no one had any idea who had been buried there. A few months later, a monument suddenly appeared overnight as though by magic. It read: "Julia, Our Daughter." Even with these clues, however, nobody knew the identity of the grave's occupant. Every once in a while, some unknown person placed flowers on the grave. Naudaine kept a close watch but was never able to unravel the secret. Years passed; people ceased speculating about the mysterious grave; Naudaine himself died; a new caretaker, M.P. Alpha, took over. Then one day in summer 1898, Samuel McWilliams, an eighty-year-old from Borden, approached Alpha and revealed the truth: Julia had been the illegitimate daughter of McWilliams and his girlfriend. The three had lived at Seymour. When the little girl died, the father had transported the body to Charlestown at night, dug the grave and buried the child himself while all prying eyes were asleep. Months later, he returned to erect a gravestone. He had made many midnight trips to the grave over the years in order to leave flowers. The elderly man told the story to Alpha because he knew that he had not much time left. When McWilliams died soon afterward, he was buried near Julia—his daughter.

A STAND-UP KIND OF GUY

Reverend James Hart had been the pastor of his Baptist church at Folsomville for fifty-five years when he died at age seventy-six. Perhaps because he loved his congregation so much—or perhaps because he just wanted to give them a severe case of the creeps—Reverend Hart's final wish was that his body be propped up behind the pulpit as three other ministers gave his funeral oration. His desire was carried out to the letter, and when parishioners attended the funeral on February

21, 1904, their former preacher stood in his casket, which leaned upright against a back wall, and stared out at them with glassy, unseeing eyes. "This was the strangest funeral ever known," remarked the local paper. "While ministers endowed with life and animation spoke the burial rites, the services were practically conducted by the dead, for every eye was fastened upon the half-reclining corpse that occupied the pulpit."

A SENSITIVE FELLOW

When George Saberton died at his Jeffersonville home on October 17, 1905, one vital statistic on his burial permit had to be left blank: his date of birth. For reasons known only to Saberton, his entire life he refused to reveal either his age or the day he was born. Even his wife Catherine didn't know. All that was known for certain was that he had been born in England and moved to Madison, Indiana, when he was about eleven, and then had moved to Chicago when fifteen. A few months after that, he moved to Jeffersonville, where he remained the rest of his life. He was estimated to be about sixty-five years old. He was buried in Madison, where his tombstone presumably bears a death date but no birth date.

A Hater of Pianos and Organs

Eli Thornburg, a wealthy farmer who lived near New Burlington, was no music lover. When he died in July 1907, he left his property to his daughter Ella and her husband, John Taylor, on the condition that they never have a piano or organ in their house. Should they ever fall prey to the "piano or organ craze," as Thornburg put it, all the property would revert to other heirs.

He Wrote His Own Epitaph

Many moons ago, John Harmon explored the wilderness at Monroe, near Jeffersonville. One day, a rattlesnake bit his leg. Harmon, realizing that town was too far away to seek help and that he was doomed, took a knife and carved his own epitaph on a nearby beech tree: "John Harmon died here from the bite of a rattlesnake." He followed this with the date and a few extra lines requesting that he be buried on the spot. His body was found a few days later, and the finders did as they were told. The tree still stood as of 1898, but only the first line of the epitaph was readable.

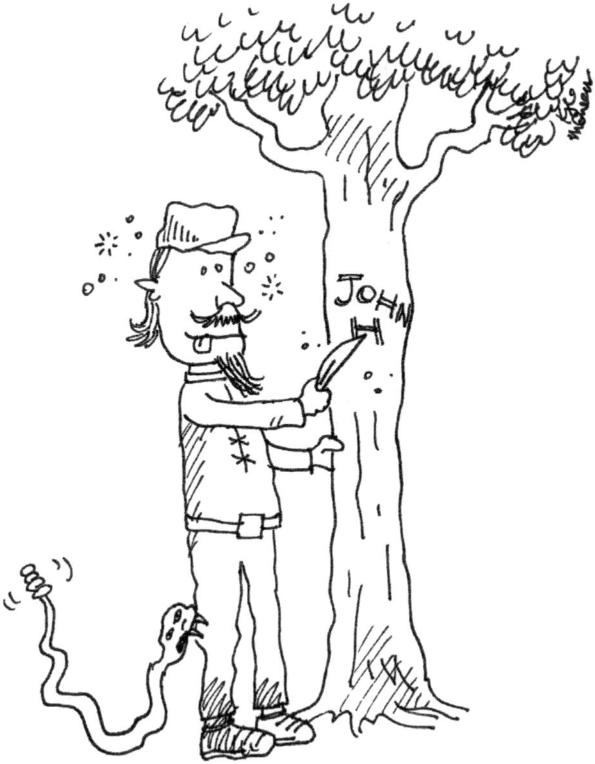
JOHN
H

THE BACHELOR'S WARNING

Hugh DeWitt of Lafayette was a lifelong bachelor—which was a considerable length of time, since he died at age ninety-three on February 13, 1908. He was buried beneath a tombstone that bore the following epitaph, which he had written himself:

A bachelor lies beneath this sod
Who disobeyed the laws of God;
Advice to others here I give,
Don't live a batch as I did live.

Buried Treasure

W.H. Hardin, described as "one of the oldest and wealthiest residents of Floyd County," had an eccentric distrust of banks. It was common knowledge among Hardin's family and friends that he had hidden a considerable amount of money *somewhere* on his farm, located twelve miles from New Albany, but nobody knew exactly where. As he lay on his deathbed in August 1892, he tried to reveal the location of his money and his will but was too weak to do so. Unfortunately for his relatives, he slipped into unconsciousness before he could spill the beans. A similar incident with a happier ending occurred in Knox County in 1913. As Abraham Hoagland lay on his deathbed, he told his family that he had buried gold on his farm, but he expired before he gave its location. For six weeks his family dug all over his 160-acre farm until, on November 23, someone uncovered a crock containing $2,500 in gold coins. That would be over $50,000 in modern currency.

In March 1900, John Wise of Harrison County had a lucky day when he dug in the foundation of an old house that had burned down on his farm and unearthed a kettle of antebellum gold coins worth an estimated $2,000. No one in the vicinity could even remember who had originally occupied the burned-down house.

James Griffin, a rich Grant County eccentric, died in the 1870s. Since he was known to have had a large amount of money at the time of his passing that was never found, rumors spread that it had been buried somewhere on his farm. For the next thirty years, his family noticed mysterious holes appearing on their land, made by treasure seekers digging furtively by the light of the moon. As far as anyone knows, the treasure (if any) was never located.

While plowing beneath a majestic poplar tree on land he was renting from Mollie Carr in summer 1903, George W. Baldock uncovered a tin box full of corroded gold and silver Spanish coins. At least, that's what he told some of the people around Charlestown. But when Miss Carr insisted that she be given a share of the loot, Baldock changed his story and said that he had found only a few coins of negligible value. On the other hand, it was said that he had recently inquired into buying a team of horses. When the seller asked if he could pay in cash, Baldock said that he certainly could and added that he could buy the seller's farm as well. There were also rumors that Baldock had suddenly started talking about purchasing land in Oklahoma. One man claimed that when he inspected the site where the alleged treasure was found, he saw a box-shaped hole in the ground crammed full of dirt clods. Miss Carr must have decided that her tenant farmer had only been joking, as she dropped the matter, but some asserted that Baldock had indeed found the money and simply put it "out of the way."

When Wilbur Walters plowed up $1,000 in $10 and $20 gold coins, at least he knew where it came from. The money had been buried on the Brown County farm by Walters's father a half century before. He had died before revealing the location of his hidden treasure. When Walters unearthed it on March 27, 1907, the coins were worth considerably more than the land itself.

Yet another Indiana farmer who plowed up riches was William Johnson, who lived near Fredonia. In July 1908, Johnson found not only seventy-nine $2.50 gold pieces in a

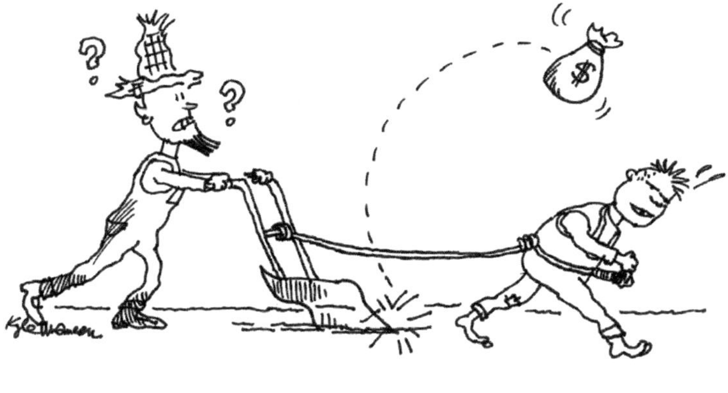

leather pouch, but also the skeleton of the original owner. The theory was that the man had drowned in the nearby Ohio River some years before and then had been washed ashore and gradually buried under layers of sediment.

George Phipps ran a lodging house on the state highway at Marion. He kept his money stashed in a box. On the night he died, his elderly widow ran outside during a ferocious storm and returned several hours later, sopping wet. Was her peculiar deed a spontaneous expression of her grief? Perhaps, but most people thought she had gone to bury the cashbox. She refused to discuss the matter and later died without telling anyone the location of the treasure, if treasure there was. Thus began the Legend of Phipps's Gold. Over the years, many an adventurer dug on the Phipps farm without success—until February 1914, when a man working the land for its then current owner unearthed a box containing $1,500 in gold and silver and a gold watch.

Then there is the legend of a certain silver mine that was fiction from start to finish. The legend began with John Work, an ironworker originally from Pennsylvania, who settled near what is now Charlestown about 1804. He built a large gristmill that was patronized by settlers and Indians. The latter group tended to pay with chunks of silver ore, claiming that they had a nearby secret mine. (Since silver is not native to southern Indiana, cooler heads have theorized that the local tribes got the precious metal by trading with distant tribes.) One old chief told Work that the Indians had decided to seal up the mine's entrance permanently. Work, believing every word of what was probably intended as a tall tale, spent the rest of his life in a fruitless search for the fabled mine. After Work died in 1832, there were plenty of credulous folk ready and eager to pick up where he left off, and a list of the men who sought the mine sounds like a who's who of early Hoosier pioneers. Searchers used methods ranging from the scientific to the exotic, including divining rods and attempts to consult the spirits of dead Indians. By 1891, the urban legend (or should we say frontier legend?) of the silver had permutated; instead of the silver being in a mine hidden by Indians, it was claimed that the silver had been buried by French monks early in the nineteenth century. As with the lost Beale treasure in Virginia and Swift's Silver Mine in Kentucky, thousands of people have spent time and money over the decades looking for the Indiana silver mine, but no one has ever found so much as a lead washer. It is alleged to be in the vicinity of Fourteen Mile Creek in Clark County.

Grave Robbers Galore

As the Rufus Cantrell story indicates, Indiana lore bursts with stories about grave robbers because the eager patronage of Indianapolis medical schools kept these peculiar tradesmen as busy as a modern *New York Times* ombudsman issuing apologies and retractions. Here, for your reading pleasure, are more true tales of tomb raiding. Brace yourself!

The Grave Robber's Comeuppance, or: The Corpse's Revenge

(Note: If you happen to be eating, or have recently eaten, you are advised to skip ahead to the next story. For that matter, you might want to go to the next chapter.)

Sarah Platts, a young lady who lived near South Bend, died of the dreaded disease tuberculosis in 1879. She was laid to rest in a country cemetery about eight miles from the city. Not long afterward, Fred Auer, a farmer who lived near the graveyard, found a human jawbone. An investigation indicated that her plot had been disturbed. The grave was opened. Most of Miss Platts was still there, but significantly, her head was missing.

Suspicion centered on Gordon Truesdale, described as a "handsome, broad-shouldered fellow with a fair education, but lazy and shiftless." He lived with his wife and four little daughters on a farm in the vicinity. Truesdale was a firm believer in phrenology, a fashionable pseudoscience of the time that held that an individual's personality and intelligence could be determined by the placement of the bumps on his head. Yes, really. Truesdale sometimes lectured on the subject at local schoolhouses and occasionally was heard to remark that his life's ambition was to own a collection of human skulls for further study. Suspicions against Truesdale solidified in March 1880, when the amateur phrenologist went to the doctor with an interesting question: is it possible to be poisoned by handling a corpse? (Apparently, he did not explain exactly why he wanted to know.) The physician answered with an emphatic "Yes," and Truesdale left his office visibly disturbed.

Immediately, Truesdale came down with a litany of horrifying symptoms. His nose hurt; he thought he had come down with erysipelas, which, according to my medical dictionary, is "an acute, febrile infectious disease, caused by a specific streptococcus, characterized by diffusely spreading deep-red inflammation of the skin or mucous membranes." He treated himself with bread and milk poultices, to no effect. His face swelled and within three days his head was twice its normal size "and lost all semblance of human shape." A doctor made a house call and found his patient of bad cheer:

> [Truesdale's] *lips were drawn by the tension of the skin, and writhed themselves away from the teeth in unceasing pain. The cuticle across the bridge of the nose and over the forehead was so distended with the mattery substance underneath that it seemed as if it must burst every moment. The eyes were swollen almost to bursting from their sockets, and were turned with pain until hardly anything but the whites could be seen.*

"It was evident," says a contemporary account with calm restraint, "that a terrible poison was slowly, but surely, permeating the man's whole system." The description of what happened next defies paraphrase, and I wouldn't even if I could:

> *The physician…cut open his skin from about the center of the nose almost to the roots of the hair, and then made another cut across the forehead almost from temple to temple. From these incisions there oozed a mass of loathsome, detestable putrescence so terrible in its stench*

> *that the attendants, save one, ran from the house. Other incisions were made in different parts of the scalp, from which the hair had been shaved, and from these this terribly offensive matter oozed constantly, until the swelling was reduced and the head and face seemed nearly their nominal size.*

The doctor attempted to clean the incisions by injecting water into them. When water was forced into the cut in the forehead, it came gushing out of the incisions in the scalp. An attendant theorized that "all the flesh between the skin and bone had turned to corruption and ran out." Truesdale was probably wishing that he had taken up checkers as a pastime rather than grave robbery.

The doctor told Truesdale that he could not possibly survive his ghastly malady, whereupon the dying man confessed to his nine-months-pregnant wife that he had indeed opened Sarah Platts's grave, cut around her neck with a knife and then yanked and twisted her head off. He had removed the jawbone and cavalierly tossed it aside, having had no use for it in his phrenological studies. Truesdale had had a sore on his nose when he robbed the grave and after handling the diseased corpse had absentmindedly touched the raw spot, thus infecting himself with what sounds like the most virulent contagion in the history of medicine. His confession ended with a clincher: he told his wife that he had hidden the skull under some straw in a barn manger. The skull was found exactly as advertised and returned to the Platts family. Let's hope they were good sports about it.

The last three wretched days of Truesdale's life made everything that came before seem like a Sunday school picnic:

> *Not only was his person offensive to the eye, but the odor and heat of his breath was so offensive that it was impossible for the attendants to wait on* [him] *properly. The breath was so poisonous that when one of the attendants held his hand six inches from the dying man's mouth it stung the flesh like hundreds of nettles. Those who waited upon him were obliged to wear gloves, as it was impossible to wash the odor from their hands. The day he died his flesh was so rotten that it seemed as if it would drop from the bones if touched, and his eyes actually decayed until they became entirely sightless.*

A coffin lay in wait to receive its repulsive burden; the nervous doctor ordered the attendants to clap Truesdale in it the very moment he died and bury him as quickly as humanly possible. When the Death Angel at last brought relief to the grave desecrator, the attendants were so afraid to touch him that they used his bedsheets to lower him into his coffin. They wasted no time screwing on the lid and sending for a wagon.

Despite these precautions, the horror show was not yet quite over. Gas built up within Truesdale's body and caused

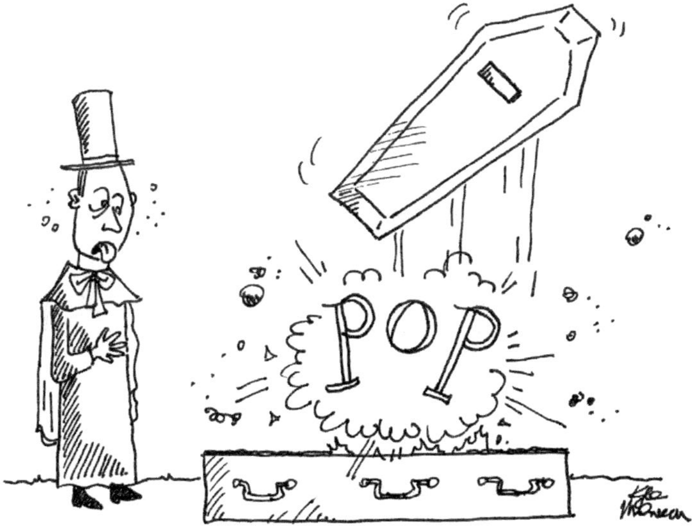

the corpse to swell so grotesquely that it burst, sending the lid flying off the coffin. The hardy attendants, who really earned their pay that day, put the lid back on and secured it with a strap. The coffin was loaded onto the wagon and taken to Truesdale's open grave in the cemetery; once there, the cadaver's explosive gas sent the lid airborne for a second time. The body continued its sinister swelling before the terrified eyes of assembled attendants and gawkers. Enough was enough; by this point in the proceedings, the body reeked so villainously that no one could bear to get close enough to put the lid back on. The lidless coffin was lowered into the grave and covered with dirt with a speed that probably set a record of some sort. It is only a wonder that the earth did not reject Truesdale's body. The mockery of a funeral was finished, and everyone went home with a great story to tell over dinner.

The day after the aspiring collector of crania was consigned to the earth, his widow gave birth to their fifth daughter. But she went into labor at a neighbor's house, as fumigation had failed to alleviate the evil smell that permeated the Truesdale residence. An attendant remarked, "It still seems as if you could cut the air in that house with a knife."

Sarah Platts had had her revenge!

Proud of His Work

Most grave robbers in bygone eras had sense enough to keep quiet about their work, if for no other reason than to avoid beatings administered by the family of the deceased. Not so for Jeff Garrigus of Indianapolis, who was so proud of his profession that when he made out his will in December 1894, he promised to leave his body to the Indiana Medical College. He added a strange proviso: he insisted that his body be dissected by students, after which they were to display his skeleton propped up in a standing position with his right hand on the handle of a shovel and his left foot resting on the blade. He wanted the shovel to be polished and have the words "Jeff Garrigus, resurrectionist" painted on it in big black letters just to make sure that no one who beheld his remains would have any doubt about what he had done for a living. "[T]he faculty has promised to carry out his wishes to the letter," assured a contemporary newspaper report.

RANDOM RESURRECTIONIST RECOUNTINGS

John Pixley of Memphis, Indiana, age twenty-six, suffered from an ailment no doctor could diagnose. Before he died in February 1896, puzzled physicians asked Pixley if they could dissect his body after death. He agreed, but his family had other ideas; after Pixley died, his shotgun-toting father kept a vigil near his son's grave in Bunker Hill Cemetery. He started keeping watch on February 23; he gave up and went home on March 5, completely exhausted and convinced that by then his son had decomposed to the point where it would no longer be of interest to anatomists. Two days later, the doctors had the last laugh: passersby found the grave open and the coffin bereft of its contents.

At least the motive behind the snatching of John Pixley made sense. On August 9, 1893, the body of nineteen-year-old Myrtle Lambert, described as "a highly accomplished young woman of Mooresville," was laid to rest, or so everyone thought. Three days later, someone noticed that her grave had been disturbed. An investigation proved that her coffin had been pried open "and her body horribly mutilated." No one could fathom who had done it or why.

Adam Spieth Jr., like John Pixley's father, did not trust medical students to let his wife's corpse rest in peace in Jeffersonville's Walnut Ridge Cemetery. As she lay dying, Mrs. Spieth wrote a twelve-page note arranging her funeral, including details ranging from the clothing she wished to wear to where she wanted the casket placed to the names of the preacher and pallbearers. Most of all, she was concerned that her body would be abstracted by anatomists. Her husband made a solemn vow that it would not. After her death in late September 1898, he spent ten nights guarding her mausoleum. He would sit in the doorway of the tomb, wrapped in a laprobe for warmth and cradling a shotgun, often taking a break to peer at his late wife's face by lamplight. This sight must have frozen the marrow of anyone who passed the graveyard at night.

Grave robbing became so prevalent in Indiana that stories about the depredations unseated the reason of a Bedford stonecutter with the workplace-appropriate name Will Rock. Rock's child had died in summer 1902, and he became obsessed with the fear that someone had stolen it from its resting place. The crazed man went to Green Hill Cemetery on May 18, 1903, and threatened the sexton with lingering death if he did not open the grave. The sexton took too long performing this action, so the maniac grabbed the tools and did the digging himself. When he reached the coffin, he pulled it up out of the hole and opened it. What happened next? As the press told it: "Clasping the remains of his dead child, [he] called it loudly, and in his frenzy tore its teeth from its gums with his mouth." But let us close the curtain on this unpleasant scene!

Long after legislation was passed allowing medical schools an allotment of bodies for dissection, Indianans feared that body snatchers were going to come for their loved ones. On May 25, 1912, for example, 852-pound Chauncey Morian passed away in Elwood. His widow believed that medical students would want to examine him due to his unique body type, so she refused to bury him. She contemplated cremation but changed her mind. The health authorities, not unreasonably, insisted that she dispose of her husband's body in *some* fashion, but as late as June 3, the body remained aboveground. Whatever became of it, I do not know.

BATTLE FOR THE BONES

Reverend John A. Pittinger of Delaware County told people that he was going to die soon, even though he seemed to be the picture of health. Several weeks later, in early December 1904, his prediction came true. He was taken to Union Chapel Cemetery for burial.

The reverend's brothers, Paul and Marion, were wary. Grave robbers had pilfered bodies from the cemetery three times recently, and the odd nature of the preacher's demise made him a perfect object of curiosity for the inquiring minds of medical students. It was decided to keep a furtive watch over Pittinger's burial site just in case the thieves had no respect for a man of the cloth. The brothers hid in a vacant house with a good view of the cemetery. They were wise to do so because about 2:00 a.m. on the morning of December 5, they saw two buggies making their way into the graveyard as silently as it was possible for two buggies to be at such an unholy hour. Four men with shovels emerged and went straight to the Pittinger grave. Paul and Marion opened fire on the body snatchers; the body snatchers fired back; there followed a veritable shootout, with the grave robbers ducking behind gravestones for cover. In the confusion, two of the marauders climbed over the cemetery fence. As they ran, they were rescued by the other members of their party, who had managed to make their way back to the buggies. The morning light revealed blood on a gravestone, indicating that one of the grave robbers had been hit. They had failed to retrieve Pittinger's body, but perhaps the surviving ghouls got to sell one of their own.

A SISTER'S VIGIL

Jesse Coe, an outlaw, was shot by officers while resisting arrest on August 25, 1908. He had been wanted for shooting two Indianapolis policemen in September 1906. He was sent to the black Odd Fellows Cemetery in Glasgow, Kentucky, for burial and was followed in short order by his mentally deranged sister, Cassy Rasberry. Having heard rumors that grave robbers were coming to retrieve her brother, she made it her business to sit in the graveyard at night, allegedly heavily armed and bathed in the soft glow of lantern-light. "The cemetery is in a lonely place," remarked a reporter, "and the sight of the woman sitting by the grave is nerve-racking to those who do not know of her belief and not familiar with the facts." Some people avoided passing the cemetery at night for fear she might mistake them for a ghoul and have at them.

HIS OWN PRIVATE CEMETERY

Tod Dew, one of the wealthiest citizens in southern Indiana, was troubled by the prospect of grave robbers stealing the body of his son. He was rich enough to do something about it. As the owner of about nine hundred acres of Kirkland Township, he set aside three to make a private family cemetery on his farm. He hired an architect and a landscaper from Indianapolis to design and beautify the place. Dew's cemetery was surrounded by a stone fence with an iron gate in it and was guarded day and night. It was designed so that only five people should ever be buried there: Dew himself, his wife, his son and daughter and Dew's brother.

THE DESERTED MEDICAL SCHOOL

Readers may have deduced after reading about Rufus Cantrell, King of the Ghouls, that although medical schools were founded with the aim of improving the quality of life for suffering humanity, such establishments were regarded with suspicion. For one thing, they were notorious patrons of grave robbers. For another, medical school students were infamous for committing unseemly pranks employing bits and pieces of dissected cadavers. And then there were incidents like the one described below.

For years, the five-room building located at the corner of Fifth and Vine Streets in Evansville was used as a medical college and public dispensary. For some unknown reason, it was abandoned in February 1885, and the staff who had used it did not have the courtesy to clean up when they left. Nor, it appears, did they bother locking the doors. As a result, for a while anyone who felt like it could enter at will and drink in the many, many horrors of the place, which the *Evansville Daily Courier* called a "monstrous disregard for the commonest dictates of humanity…An outrage too abhorrent for characterization." Fortunately, the details were preserved for us by a reporter, who accompanied the chief of police when the latter examined the place on February 23. "On entering the yard in the rear of the building," writes our deadpan hero, "parts of female anatomy were found scattered around promiscuously." (A second squeamish reporter referred to these decorations as "the nameless portions of three females.") The tour of the place then went downhill.

The building smelled of advanced decay despite the fact that it was wintertime. One second-story room was used to deposit remains after dissection; there, forty-five dissected bodies lay on the floor, "a scene of horror which must be seen to be fully appreciated." Some bodies still had flesh adhering; some were headless; others were lying about "in every conceivable position." It was evident also that famished rats had considered the room their own private buffet. The occasional bat or owl flitting about added to the Gothic atmosphere.

In the dissection room itself were five tables, four of which leaned against the wall, "covered with blood, hair and other offal that adhered to them." The room was full of human anatomical specimens—most the fruits of the labors of grave robbers, or "Jerry Crunchers," as the *Courier* put it, referring to the resurrectionist in Dickens's *A Tale of Two Cities*. Dismembered segments of individuals were strewn across the floor of this room. In the corner stood a shiny new coffin that showed no signs of having been placed underground; the inference was that some unethical undertaker had sold the corpse to the medical school instead of burying it. The faculty and students had also left behind many tools of their trade, including worn-out knives and saws. In an adjoining room were three corpses that had been cast aside as useless. The place must have had the laziest janitor *ever*.

Most rooms in the building had body parts scattered on the floors, as though Ed Gein had been the interior decorator; the reporter noted that in many cases, amputated feet still wore their original owners' socks. Every room was filled with clothing taken from the bodies of their unwilling donors. What the medical students had intended to do with the clothes, no one knew. The building's former occupants had singular notions about landscaping as well as interior decorating: "Even on the [side]walks about the building may be found some portions of both male and female, which were evidently thrown out with the intention that passers-by might view them." The reporter concluded:

> *It seems that those who have been in charge have cared very little about the proper disposition of the remains, which to leave for a time would result in the starting point of pestilence. Citizens are very indignant, and steps will be taken immediately to see that the building, which is owned by the county, is thoroughly cleansed and fumigated, and, if possible, to punish the parties guilty of this public indecency.*

To make matters worse—if that were even possible—the police failed to secure the building after news of its condition hit the papers; an inspection the next day revealed that vandals had treated the deserted building as if it were their very own house of horrors. Intruders blessed with an unhealthy sense of humor had intentionally posed remains in order to increase their shock value. Notable was "one brawny and unsightly carcass of a Negro" placed in a sitting position, leaning on one elbow, chin in hand as though in deep thought. The top of his head had been sawed off, and he sat with "grinning mouth wide open, facing the door, with its eyeless sockets looking menacingly at anyone coming in." The remains of a woman peered sightlessly out a window. She was held in place by a headless man; in the background bodies large and small "had been dragged from other portions of the room for the sole purpose seemingly of making the scene more repulsive and disgusting than that of the day previous." Worse, various chunks of humans that the reporter had seen the

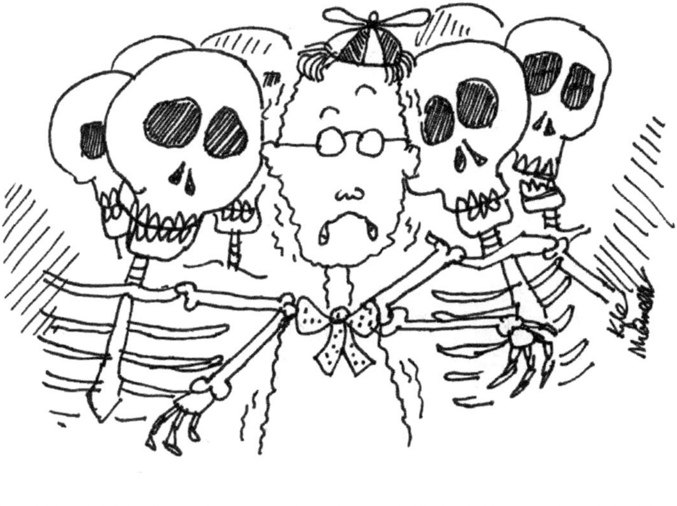

day before were now missing, taken by practical jokers who displayed them in various parts of Evansville where people did not particularly wish to see them. A skull was found perched atop a hitching post near the courthouse; another such "grim emblem of death" was discovered peeking out of a hole in a barrel used to cover a fireplug.

On February 25, after three excruciating days, a judge at last gave the sheriff orders to guard the deserted building and kick out any vandals or thrill-seekers found within. All of the remains discovered on the premises were placed in a large box and given a Christian burial in Locust Hill Cemetery. It appears that the guilty medical school faculty and students were never caught. It is not certain what would have been done with them even if they had been found, for they had broken no laws that were on the books in Indiana at the time. Allegedly, some of the persons responsible for the building's filthy condition and abandonment were members of the city's Board of Health.

Life Is Like That Sometimes

Oh, Rats!

One seemingly benign day in 1872, Jefferson Miller of Jeffersonville was busily feeding a threshing machine in his barn when he beheld a rat scampering across the floor. Distracted by the rodent, Miller neglected to watch what he was doing and the machine tore off his left hand.

Flash forward to February 1887. Once again, Miller was in his barn feeding the threshing machine, with less dexterity than previously; once again, an insolent rat ran by. No doubt feeling somewhat akin to Captain Ahab when that maimed literary character finally met up with Moby Dick, Miller kicked at the rat. He lost his balance and fell against the machine, which tore off his right hand.

TRACKS IN THE ROCK

The town of Franklin faced a puzzle in November 1879, during the construction of its courthouse. Large rocks were mined at a quarry at Vernon and brought to the worksite. One three- by six-foot stone had a dozen human footprints embedded in one side. As described by a contemporary witness, "Some of them were misshapen, as if having been made in soft clay and crowded by contiguous tracks, but many were in almost perfect formation." Even weirder: "None were barefoot tracks, but evidently made by fashionably-shaped shoes." Weirder still: there were also a couple of bovine tracks. The tracks were not of recent origin; in some of them there had been "an after-formation of rocks," which were easily removed with a chisel. The witness concluded his report: "The question that naturally arises is, who were the people that, wearing shoes with fashionably high heels and well-rounded shanks, made their tracks in the soft blue clay that afterward solidified into stone?" A week after the mysterious rock was found, it was given to the county as a present by the firm of Farman and Pierce, the courthouse contractors.

INDIANA'S SKUNK FARMS

In the late nineteenth century, skunk farming was one of Indiana's great underground industries—underground in the sense that few people knew, or for that matter wanted to know, that skunk farms even existed. In summer 1879, an *Indianapolis News* reporter spoke with Mr. Lewark, a proprietor of skunk-related products, who explained that the animal's value lay in the oil that could be procured from its skin. The polecat impresario claimed that people from all walks of life took skunk oil for rheumatism and that "it never fails to cure." Lewark showed a pint flask of the genuine article to the journalist, who wrote that it was "the color of linseed oil" and, to his great surprise, it "had no more and no worse odor than lard oil." A normal-sized skunk skin could yield four ounces of oil; if luck was with the pelt processor, but not with the skunk, a pint could be gained. Lewark said that he bought pelts of the loveliest and fattest, and therefore most valuable, skunks for prices ranging from $1.75 to $2.00 apiece (in modern currency those prices would be about $40 and $45). A low-class, common hide went for $0.20 (modern equivalent, about $4.45). The skunk baron further told the reporter, "I handled 20,000 skunk skins last year, nearly all of which were caught in Indiana…I've been a fur buyer for forty-two years, and there are more skunks in this state now than ever was." Since the average mama skunk has three to seven babies at a time, and few predators are so foolish as to take on a skunk, there was no danger of the aromatic beasts going extinct.

Once the oil was extracted from a skunk hide, said hide could also be used to make fur coats, muffs, trimmings for

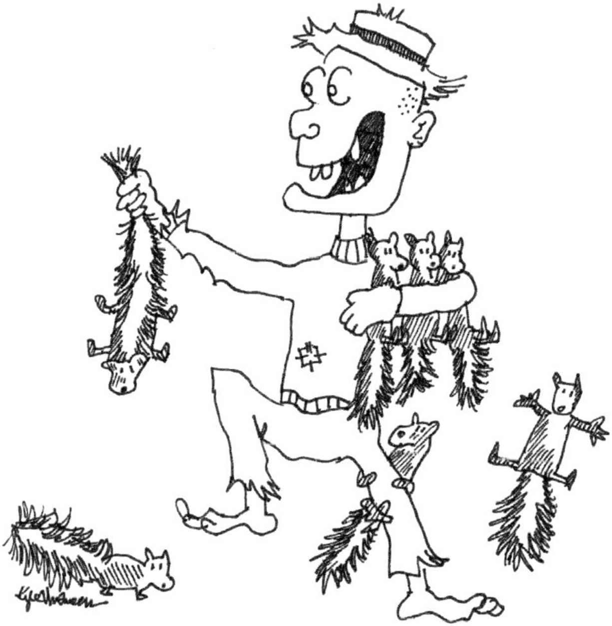

clothes and carriage robes. Naturally, fashion-conscious consumers were not told that the high-priced clothing they were purchasing was made of skunk fur; the product was known by a variety of charming euphemisms, such as "fitch" and "American sable."

Since polecats were so valuable, it's no wonder that some entrepreneurs established farms on which they specially bred, slaughtered and sold an animal that most people would willingly walk five miles to avoid. By 1901, according to one old newspaper article, "so many skunk farms have sprung up that a trust has been formed. It is said there are six large skunk farms in Indiana, the principal one being on the Walmer farm in Clinton County." The pelts were still going for two dollars apiece.

Let us pause for a moment and doff our hats in silent tribute to those souls from long ago who were brave enough, and sufficiently desperate for money, to work on skunk farms. They still exist, though not on a large scale, and with the purpose of breeding the animals as pets.

CONVICTED BY A DREAM

In the 1840s, a fellow named Foxworthy lived on Walnut Street in Louisville, Kentucky. He was wise enough to be a hard worker and save his money. He was unwise enough to salt it away in a trunk in his apartment instead of putting it in a bank. He was unwiser still in letting the latter fact become generally known. Mr. Whittinghill, a blacksmith who resided in the same boardinghouse, wanted desperately to marry a certain young lady, but had to have money in order to trick her into thinking he was well off. He knew that Foxworthy had $100 in cash and was determined to get it.

On the morning of July 3, 1847, Whittinghill invited Foxworthy to go hunting with him in the forest just outside Jeffersonville. The two crossed the river into Indiana in a skiff, the unwary Foxworthy armed with a gun and his so-called friend with a club made of the finest hickory. They entered the woods, where Foxworthy found out too late that he was the only game that interested Whittinghill. He brained Foxworthy and then hid the club and corpse in a thicket. Returning to the boardinghouse, he struck as nonchalant an air as he could, not an easy thing to do since many people had seen the two hunters leave Louisville and only one return—without his club. When asked the obvious question, he replied that Foxworthy had found work in Jeffersonville and had decided to live there. He also showed off a paper allegedly signed by Foxworthy, requesting that his trunk be turned over to his dear pal Whittinghill. The boardinghouse proprietor didn't believe a word of it and refused to hand it over. Whittinghill lost his nerve and promptly disappeared.

The morning after the murder, Joseph Nagle of Jeffersonville was engaged in constructing oyster boats at Port Fulton. As he looked around the woods for building materials, he literally tripped over the mound containing the previous day's corpse. Nagle had no idea whose body he had found and ran to the authorities, who put it on public display at a market house. Hundreds of people came to see it—while doing their shopping, I guess—including the Louisville boardinghouse owner, who identified it as Foxworthy and expressed his belief that the missing Whittinghill was the murderer. The police believed he was correct and soon had the protesting suspect in custody in Jeffersonville.

In those days, DNA evidence was unknown and fingerprinting was years in the future. Many had seen Whittinghill leaving Louisville with a club, but without the murder weapon a conviction was unlikely. Scores of searchers combed the woods for it, to no avail. But one of them, Thomas Morgan, had a dream in which he met the ghost of Foxworthy, who led him to a swamp and showed him the club hidden under a rotten log. When Morgan awoke, he hurried into the forest and wandered until he found a piece of land that, to his amazement, matched exactly what he had seen in his dream. He located the log and, exploring under it with a stick, found the murder weapon bespattered with brains, blood and hair.

Whittinghill received the death penalty, but he "died from remorse" several months later in jail while waiting for his sentence to be carried out.

THE HEROIC NEWSBOY

An Indiana hero turned up in the less-than-likely form of Billy Rugh, a young vagrant with a withered leg and no family. Rugh had drifted to the city of Gary in 1910 and decided to stay there and sell newspapers for a living. The cheerful Rugh quickly became a local favorite, but no one realized that he had the stuff of greatness until Ethel Smith, age eighteen, was fearsomely burned when her fiancé wrecked his motorcycle in September 1912. Rugh, who had never met Smith, offered to allow doctors to amputate his crippled leg so that the girl's life might be saved with a skin graft. The operation was a success for Miss Smith but fatal to Rugh; the ether used to render him unconscious irritated his lungs and resulted in pneumonia. On the morning of October 13, Rugh remarked while lying in his hospital bed, "I don't care so much about death if she gets well." Then he said, "I guess I turned out to be some good after all," turned his face to the wall and died.

When Ethel Smith was informed, she cried, "I am so sorry. He gave his life for me and I could do nothing for him." Rugh was sent to Orion, Illinois, for burial, but not before Gary held a funeral fit for a statesman. The *Chicago Tribune* reported that fifteen thousand people—a third of the city's population—paid their respects. No building was large enough to accommodate them, so the funeral had to be held in the street. Afterward, plans were announced to erect a statue of the heroic newsboy; people from faraway places such as Boston, including millionaires and fellow newsboys, sent contributions, and a benefit show was held in Chicago. The granite marker memorializing Rugh still stands on the lawn of Gary's Memorial Auditorium.

But the greatest testament to Rugh's valor and selflessness is that Ethel Smith lived to become a wife and mother.

INDIANA ECCENTRICS

Every town has one person who is pointed out as the "local character." In some towns, it seems that a number of people compete for the honor. Here are the stories of notable Indiana eccentrics.

Few things fire the imagination like the archetypical "eccentric millionaire." Patrick Huncheon, an early founder of the town of LaCrosse, adequately fulfilled both the adjective and the noun. When he died at age seventy on June 14, 1897, he was the wealthiest landowner in northern Indiana. He spent his last thirty years living with his equally strange brother; they had refused to speak a word to each other for decades.

An authentic wild man was captured in a church at Poplar Grove, near Kokomo, on January 21, 1899. Somehow, he had broken in and was found walking on all fours between the pews. Despite the winter chill, he was practically nude, but covered with shaggy hair. He was immensely strong and seemed to be over eighty years old. The only thing he could tell the police was that his name was Jacobson.

Another wild man, this one uncaught, terrorized Clark County in September 1899. He lurked about New Market, Marysville and Otisco and was described as wearing only a shirt and a ratty pair of trousers. He greeted one person by trying to bash his head with a club.

Phoebe Meeks was famed as "the Brookville recluse." When she was young, she had had a beau, but one Sunday in autumn 1835, she left her boyfriend's company and walked home without a word of explanation. She refused to open the door when he came calling that evening, and she never left her house again until she was carried out as a corpse in November 1900. She took to the grave the secret she had kept for sixty-five years. The train depot was only a block from her house, yet she never saw a train in her life. She was not insane, her obituary noted; she was widely read and intelligent. "The few who were admitted to see her were charmed with her vivacity and brilliant conversational powers. While she would not cross the threshold of her home, she took an intense interest in local affairs, and many were the arguments in local matters which she was called upon to settle." Today, we would recognize Phoebe Meeks as likely having agoraphobia. But in 1900, the big mystery was why she would abandon such a fine catch of a boyfriend. Her death notice dropped some hints as to his identity:

> *Her lover was a prominent man. For years he sought to wean her from her seclusion, but she would* [have] *none of it. He married, and in the far West his wife died. Again and again he came back to his Indiana home, but never was he permitted to see her. His last visit was in 1897, when, as the bearer of the first electoral vote of Utah to Congress, he stopped off while returning. Two years ago he died.*

The title "oddest man in Indiana" was bestowed upon John Simon Covert, a woman-hating old bachelor who lived alone near Otisco in the early years of the twentieth century. So isolated was he—and determinedly so—that he had no idea what was going on in the world outside of his farm. He read neither newspapers nor almanacs and owned no calendar; therefore, he never even knew what day of the week it was. He knew no holidays and only knew by the disposition of the weather what season it was. He had no clock and could only estimate the time of day by the position of the sun. If he needed to know the precise time, he had to travel some distance to visit a neighbor who possessed a timepiece. He took meals at no set time, but rather when his stomach told him it was time to eat.

Another old bachelor who eschewed the company of women, Isaac "Ike" Perry of Slate Cut, near Jeffersonville, made news when he supervised the construction of his own tomb and monument at age ninety-four in 1904. He ordered a granite monument sixteen feet tall over his plot in Silver Creek Cemetery; in addition to the usual mundane information (name, dates of birth and death), Perry wanted the manufacturer to chisel a receipt for the monument in the granite, in order to prove to the world that he had paid for it in full. Meanwhile, Perry supervised the construction of a Bedford stone tomb and made his own coffin out of timber that he had been seasoning for a half-century. The coffin included a window and was fashioned to be wide enough to allow his body easy movement on Resurrection

Day. The cement vault was completed in October 1905. One of Perry's favorite pastimes was visiting his future tomb; he remarked that it was so solidly constructed that the devil couldn't get his body if he wanted it. Perry began using his homemade crypt for its intended purpose on September 18, 1907.

William Windell of Valley City had an obsession similar to Perry's. Because he expected his demise to come soon, in 1903 the elderly Windell spent several weeks digging his own grave in a rural cemetery, complete with a stone masonry vault at the bottom and a shelter over the hole to keep rain from pouring in. Perhaps to his disappointment, Windell failed to die. In January 1905, Windell fell on the ice while visiting relatives in Corydon, resulting in his making use of the grave he had dug himself.

LOVE FEVER

Smallpox was no small matter in the Good Old Days. It was highly contagious, often fatal, disfigured survivors and its germs could live for decades outside the human body under optimal conditions. Persons who came down with it were promptly quarantined in special places enchantingly called pesthouses. They were not to leave until either healed or deceased; it goes without saying that they were allowed no company.

All of this is background to an inspiring love story. In April 1902, Katie Trainor of Xenia, Illinois, contracted smallpox while visiting Washington, Indiana, the hometown of her boyfriend, Charley Padgett. She was hauled off to the pesthouse, where she pined away for love of Charley.

It was illegal to enter a pesthouse, but what was that to Charley? On the morning of April 18, he kicked the lock off the door and entered as though he owned the place. The nurse alerted the police, but the first officer on the scene had not sufficient nerve to enter a quarantined building. A couple of officers who had already had smallpox, and therefore were immune, stormed the building with every intention of dragging the ardent lover out. Charley produced a revolver "and defied them to attempt to separate him from the girl he loved." The officers managed to overpower and capture Padgett; they took him to the Board of Health, where he was fumigated and forcibly inoculated. Somehow, he managed to escape with a gaggle of cops on his trail, all anxious to press charges for housebreaking, carrying a concealed weapon and violating health laws.

I don't know if Katie and Charley got married, but if they did, they had a great story to tell the grandkids.

He Took His Time

On March 16, 1867, Michael Huff's stepmother sent him out to gather up the moo-cows for milking at their Danville farm. Huff disappeared without a trace but returned on March 16, 1910. By then, Huff's brother Elmer was living at the ol' homestead. The first thing Michael said after the family answered the door was that he was now ready to commence milking. During the forty-three-year interim between the assigning of the chore and the beginning of it, Huff had sneaked off to Missouri for an education and became the superintendent of the State Reform School in Kansas.

THE FEATS OF MERRIFIELD

Hammond Merrifield was widely regarded as one of the most remarkable men in LaGrange, if not in the entire United States. Despite having been completely blind since age eighteen, he built his five-room cottage entirely by himself. "The timbers are joined together perfectly," said a marveling reporter in 1902, "and there is not a single mistake or blunder in either the foundation or the superstructure." In the wintertime, Merrifield cut his own wood. He had a habit of hiding his axe after a day's labor, "and the next morning he does not experience the slightest difficulty in finding the ax." He was also able, though sightless, to find small objects on the street: "If someone lays a silver dollar on the sidewalk and tells him within fifty feet of where it is, he can easily go to that part of town and find it." Merrifield was quite the handyman with tools and could make wagons, wheelbarrows and chairs. The only thing he had trouble manufacturing was axe handles. He kept cattle and was perfectly capable of herding them through the town streets with no help whatsoever. He often traveled on foot across country to places as far away as Albion (twenty miles), and would follow railroad tracks to Wolcottville or to Sturgis, Michigan. He could identify everyone in LaGrange by voice. At age sixty, Merrifield told a reporter:

> *I have no secret. I do not know how I get along, but somehow it is natural for me to do anything that anyone else does. Instead of seeing objects I hear them. That may sound strange, but it is true. For instance, if I were to meet you on the street and you were to remain perfectly motionless I could hear you. That sense of hearing prevents me from bumping into anybody, or colliding with any object. I could hear a dead man or an inanimate object just as readily as a live man. I have worked hard for fifty years and today I do not have a stiff joint, an ache or a pain. There is just one thing that I haven't done, and that I intend to do, and that is to learn to ride a bicycle.*

A Legal Conundrum

Alfred Helton of Paynestown predicted in June 1913 that he would be dead within three months. Helton was a doctor and evidently knew what he was talking about. When he visited Bloomington on the morning of August 4, he seemed in good health, but when he returned home in the afternoon he was stricken with heart failure. Five minutes before he expired, Dr. Helton filled out his own official death certificate. He also had time to scribble a friendly note to Coroner Harris asking that no inquest be held. This created an interesting legal problem: can a death certificate filled out by the deceased be considered valid? Coroner Harris decided that it could, on the grounds that "the law does not specify that the physician in charge shall be alive when the certificate is filed."

MEN HAVE KILLED FOR LESS

Edward Morton, aka Edward Coffey, was a prisoner in the Indiana Reformatory at Jeffersonville. On August 21, 1913, he stabbed fellow convict Charles Bartle of Junction City, Kentucky, with a shoe knife. Why did he murder the poor fellow? Morton explained that he was really craving a smoke and tobacco was not allowed in the reformatory. He figured that if he killed someone, he would get sent to the State Prison, where cigarettes were permitted. As Morton said, "I guess I will be hanged, but if not I will be transferred to Michigan City, where I can get all of the tobacco I want." Given that Indiana introduced the electric chair as a means of legal punishment in September 1913, only a month after Morton's deed, it is possible that he did some smoking of an entirely different sort at the state pen.

THE JURY SYSTEM IN ACTION

George L. Ryan was on trial in Vincennes in October 1903 for assault with intention of committing murder—not a trivial charge. The jury ("made up of the best men in the county," a news report assures us) was deadlocked. How to reach a decision so they could all go home? Someone came up with this intelligent means of serving justice: each jury member put a nickel in a hat. The hat was shaken and its contents poured on a table. If most coins came up heads, Ryan would be acquitted; if tails predominated, Ryan would be convicted. Heads won, and Ryan was summarily acquitted and turned loose. The state's attorney heard about their scheme and informed the judge, who excoriated the jury and vowed to have them prosecuted. As Bob Dylan once sang, "In ceremonies of the horsemen, even the pawn must hold a grudge." No, I don't know what it means either.

IS THE ENTRANCE TO HELL IN INDIANA?

In 1834, the U.S. government sent surveyor Jeremiah Smith to explore the swampy section of Indiana around what became known as the Kankakee bottoms in LaPorte and Starke Counties. Smith began his task on May 28 and completed it on January 15, 1835. He had some unflattering things to say about the region, which he called a "miserable floating marsh," while the impassable land "beggars description." He added, "The Lord deliver me from all such places hereafter!" In his report dated June 3, 1834, Smith declared that the Kankakee River actually must be the River Styx, the Greek mythological boundary between Earth and the netherworld, and that English Lake was really the Stygian pool. The Yellow River was a gathering spot for damned souls and "The Door Prairie, and other smaller ones about it, I take to be what remains of the Elysian Fields." He wrote that he had found the spot where Charon landed his ferry to pick up the dead and had even found one of that distinguished gentleman's oars. In other words, this official government document hinted rather strongly that the entrance to Hades was located in northern Indiana. Smith was probably kidding, but perhaps he had been walking in the sun without a hat for too long.

A HORRID DISEASE

When Thomas Seaman, age thirty-three, died of a stomach ulcer at his mother's home at 602 East Maple Street, Jeffersonville, it undoubtedly came as a relief to Seaman and his relatives. It ended years of torment brought on by a bizarre disease that had first manifested itself seventeen years before. At age thirteen, Seaman's joints and muscles became perfectly rigid; his legs were immovably locked below the knees. He then developed something the physicians called osteomalacia, which was the opposite of his former illness. His bones became so soft and spongy that he was unable to stand or move. He was forced to lie in bed all day, able to move only by pulling on straps and ropes attached to his bed. Worst of all, he developed abscesses, through which pieces of bones would work their way through the surface of his skin. At first, Seaman threw these stray bits of bone away; then he decided to save them so that they could be buried with him. When the merciful end came on August 27, 1905, he was laid to rest with a box containing 122 bone fragments.

MARVELOUS GRIFFITH

"I lay claim to being the mathematical wonder of the United States," said Arthur F. Griffith. Few would have argued with him, as he had by then become nationally famous as "Marvelous Griffith" for his ability to do complicated mathematical equations mentally and accurately. He was what was then called a "lightning calculator," and his feats were the stuff of legend.

Griffith was born in Syracuse, Indiana, in 1880, and grew up in Milford. He displayed an affinity for math from early childhood, when he would count the grains of corn as he fed the family's chickens. When he went to school, he boggled his teachers' minds with his impromptu and difficult calculations. He first came to public attention in 1898. It was noted that unlike many mathematical savants, who tend to be monomaniacal, surly and socially backward, Griffith was pleasant, had a good sense of humor and was able to converse on a number of topics other than math. Like most of his kind, Griffith had a phenomenal memory. He could remember and discuss math problems he had worked out long after the fact. Unlike many math prodigies who are unable to explain how they do what they do, Griffith articulately discussed his mental "systems." According to one account, he wrote "ten short methods for addition, two for subtraction, eighty for multiplication, six for division, seventy for mensuration, and more than 400 for fractions, decimals, denominate numbers, percentage, interest, involutions, evolution, and miscellaneous propositions." He made arrangements to publish an explanation of his systems and mental shortcuts for calculation, but the book appears never to have seen the light of day.

On one occasion a skeptical financial editor asked Griffith to calculate 14,551,915,228,366,851,806,640,625 times 68,719,476,735. Ten seconds later, Griffith had the correct answer: 999,999,999,985,448,084,771,633,148,193,359,375. "I work that by my own shortcut rule—number 142—for multiplication," said Griffith, seemingly unaware that his explanation explained nothing at all to the average person. Forget billions and trillions, quadrillions and quintillions; Griffith could handle calculations up in the vigintillions (a number followed by sixty-three zeroes).

On another occasion, Griffith computed—just for the joy of it, it appears—the compound interest on a dollar at 6 percent from the time of the birth of Christ to the present. "This was the most difficult problem I have ever figured out," he remarked. "It took me a half hour." He noted that if John D. Rockefeller was worth $600 million, the compound interest he had calculated would be sufficient for more than 20,000,000,000,000,000,000,000,000,000,000,000,000,000,000,000 Rockefellers. Here are a few of the many brain teasers devised by Griffith; he did not provide the answers, as he assumed people would enjoy trying to figure them out. Have fun!

- In how many different positions can the fifty-two cards in a deck of cards be arranged? ("The number will be astounding," said Griffith, "and if one contents himself working out the problem by the old long rules I am afraid he will not get through the task soon.")
- What is the weight of the ground one mile deep under the United States?
- What numbers up to 1,000 will ever be the remainder after dividing by 1,001, if the dividend is a perfect cube? Ditto, if the dividend is a perfect fourth power?
- If all the states and territories were arranged in one row, how far would they reach and in how many different positions could they be in one row?

- How many different numbers with thirty digits will always divide 1,073,741,824 out even?
- Suppose it had rained all over the United States 17 percent of the time from the birth of Christ to the present time, raining forty-five drops to the square inch a second, and had taken 800 drops to make a pint, and we had all that water here, how much water would it make and how deep would it be?

Professors at Indiana State University took their homegrown genius to visit mathematicians at Yale who, after seeing Griffith strut his stuff, declared that he was among the dozen or so most notable prodigies in history. His skills were tested at such universities as Harvard, Chicago and Northwestern; it was found that he could raise a figure to the sixth power in eleven seconds, multiply three figures by three figures in five seconds and multiply nine figures by nine figures in eight seconds. During the Harvard test, he answered correctly every question put to him, "the fabled 'fourth dimension' alone being barred."

Arthur Griffith enjoyed having his abilities tested in less academic surroundings as well. On three occasions, he won races against adding machines; on a bet, he did the work of fourteen clerks in three hours at the state auditor's office in Springfield, Illinois. Eventually, he became a vaudeville entertainer. On Christmas Day 1911, he died of apoplexy in a hotel bed in Springfield, Massachusetts, en route to an engagement in Bridgeport, Connecticut. He was thirty-one years old.

NO SMOKING ALLOWED

Perhaps the sensible and even-tempered reader feels that antismoking zealots have gone too far; after all, recently they tried to have smoking banned *outside* public buildings as well as inside them; in some places, there was talk of banning smoking inside private residences. However, this was child's play compared to the antismoking laws enacted in Indiana over a century ago.

Do-gooders wanted to make it more difficult for boys to obtain cigarettes. In May 1905, the Indiana Senate passed a law banning the sale and use of cigarettes—more or less as a joke, according to the newspapers. When the bill went to the House, a foolhardy man employed in the tobacco industry predicted that it would never become a law "because money would be used freely to defeat it." The politicians in the House understood this to mean that they could easily be bribed. Taking umbrage at perceived slurs on their integrity, the House members passed the bill. In other words, a bill that started out as a joke became the law in Indiana due to spite.

But not only did the law prohibit the manufacture and sale of cigarettes within the state's borders, it also made the mere ownership of a cigarette a punishable crime. As might be guessed, the Anti-Cigarette Law proved immensely unpopular both within the state and without, partly because it interfered with personal liberty and partly because violators faced Draconian penalties. Within days after the law was enacted, two men in New Albany were arrested for the dire crime of owning cigarettes; one was released after his friends paid a thirty-five-dollar fine on his behalf, but the other found himself facing a thirty-five-day term in jail. In July, Edward Hammel, a traveling salesman of patent medicines, was arrested at Lafayette for smoking and given a fine of twenty-five dollars and costs. He had not sufficient funds and was sent to jail for twenty-nine days. On October 2, Chester Phillips and Charles Caesar were arrested for thoughtlessly smoking near the New Albany police station. Tobacco and papers were found on their persons, which ensured even harsher treatment: they were fined thirty-five dollars each. A number of people from out of state, who had never heard of the law, found themselves getting punished for lighting up.

The hard-luck champion appears to have been John McCormick of Marion, who on May 10 was fined thirty-seven dollars merely for having one cigarette paper in his possession. He was unable to pay and was sent to jail for *forty-seven weeks.*

William W. Lowry, an Indianapolis lawyer, was so determined to test the law's constitutionality that he entered the Marion County Courthouse defiantly puffing away on a cancer stick and informing the deputy prosecutor that he had a thousand more at his house. Lowry was indicted immediately. He made bond and returned for his trial on May 13, vowing that if found guilty he would take the case to the state Supreme Court. A jury refused to convict him.

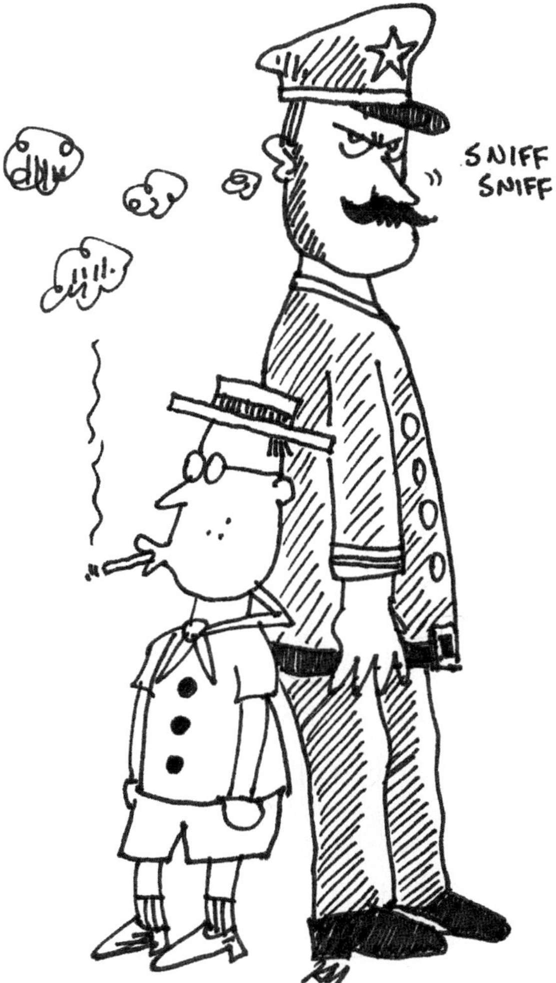
SNIFF
SNIFF

The constitutionality of the law was further tested in a more absurd fashion. E.S. Danby of Anderson wrote to Governor Hanly in late July stating that his pet chimpanzee had been addicted to the Evil Weed for years and a doctor had informed him that the chimp's health would be greatly affected, if not endangered, if he didn't get some smokes. Here was a legal dilemma, to be sure. The law said nothing specifically about non-humans. Was it, then, a violation of the law to allow a monkey to smoke? Did it set a bad example for men and boys if the primate were allowed to continue indulging his bad habit? The governor answered Mr. Danby—with, I suspect, all the dignity a governor can muster under such circumstances—that he had "no power to suspend the law in respect to chimpanzees or anyone else." As it turned out, Danby was correct: the monkey died on August 3, and the doctors who performed an autopsy found that "the tracheal muscles [were] rigid and contracted and also the intercostal and abdominal muscles [were] in a condition showing that they had been deprived of a sedative produced by cigarettes that could not be replaced by other narcotics."

The Anti-Cigarette Law engendered so much legal chaos and ill feeling that the Supreme Court of Indiana ruled on April 26, 1906, that the law was valid but construed it as "not applying in the case of a person who brings cigarettes into the state in the conduct of interstate commerce, and not forbidding persons to smoke cigarettes, but only to sell them or keep them for sale." In other words, the court determined that the law should be aimed at dealers rather than smokers, so Hoosiers again had the right to *smoke* cigarettes, but not to *sell* them. Eventually, the sale of cigarettes was again made legal. At least one person in jail for smoking, John M. Lewis of Anderson, had his conviction reversed, and the day after the Supreme Court ruling, crowds of the nicotine-famished gathered in Jeffersonville for a public smokefest. Thoughtful folks in New Albany wondered whether people who had been fined or served time for smoking were illegally prosecuted and entitled to compensation. That can of legal worms, it appears, was never opened.

Bibliography

Rufus Cantrell, King of the Ghouls

Atlanta Constitution. "Grave Robber Becomes Crazy." February 11, 1903, 1.

———. "King of Ghouls in Surly Mood." February 6, 1903, 5.

———. "Pushing the Grave Robbers." October 3, 1902, 2.

Coshocton [OH] *Daily Tribune*. "King of Ghouls Goes Onstage." August 17, 1910, 6.

Drimmer, Frederick. *Body Snatchers, Stiffs and Other Ghoulish Delights*. New York: Fawcett Gold Medal, 1981.

Elyria [OH] *Evening Telegram*. "Reformed Grave Robber Opens Revivals in Elyria." June 26, 1913, 1.

Fort Wayne [IN] *News*. "Grave Robber's Bride." December 23, 1909, 12.

———. "Grave Robbers Were Arraigned." October 27, 1902, 1.

Fort Wayne [IN] *Weekly Sentinel*. "Cantrell to Prison." May 6, 1903, 1.

———. "Ghoul Cantrell Explains Mystery." July 15, 1903, 9.

Idanha Chieftain [Soda Springs, ID]. "Ghoul Admits Crime." July 9, 1903, 3.

Louisville Courier-Journal. "Affidavits Filed…" October 3, 1902, 5.

———. "Alexander Trial Takes a New and Sudden Twist." February 8, 1903, I, 5.

———. "Another Alleged Ghoul Is Taken into Custody." January 5, 1903, 6.

———. "Another Pleads Guilty." May 8, 1903, 8.

———. "Arrests Being Made…" August 11, 1903, 5.

———. "At Least Three Years for the King of Ghouls." April 26, 1903, I, 10.

———. "Band of White Ghouls…" October 8, 1902, 2.

———. "Cantrell, the Ghoul, Convicted on Two Counts." April 24, 1903, 6.

———. "Cantrell May Reveal Fate of Miss Selvage." July 12, 1903, II, 4.

———. "Cantrell Testifies." February 5, 1903, 8.

———. "Cantrell Testifies." February 6, 1903, 3.

———. "Cantrell Testifies." March 7, 1903, 3.

———. "Deny That Bodies Have Been Brought Here…" October 6, 1902, 5.

———. "Detectives Do Not Believe Rufus Cantrell's Statement." October 1, 1903, 9.

———. "Digging Proves Truth…" October 9, 1902, 2.

———. "An Entire Day Will Be Consumed in Arguing…" 11, 1903, 2.

———. "For Killing Chinaman." April 14, 1903, 5.

———. "Found Guilty…" April 18, 1903, 4.

. "Four Cadavers…" October 14, 1902, 3.

———. "Four More Murders Charged…" August 15, 1903, 11.

———. "Ghastly Murder Described…" August 12, 1903, 2.

———. "Ghoul and Cadaver…" October 26, 1902, II, 2.

———. "Ghoul Cantrell Claims He Has Been Offered Bail…" November 21, 1902, 1.

———. "Ghoul Cantrell 'Turns Up' the Murderers." March 26, 1903, 10.

———. "Ghoul Insists He Came to Louisville…" October 25, 1902, 3.

———. "Ghoul Trials Begun at Indianapolis…" February 3, 1903, 10.

———. "Ghouls Busy in Small Cemeteries…" September 21, 1902, I, 5.
———. "Grave Robbers." November 23, 1902, III, 1.
———. "Husband Shares Price…" November 9, 1902, III, 2.
———. "Identified as One of the Ghouls." November 30, 1902, I, 5.
———. "Indiana Ghouls Now Charged With Murder." March 20, 1903, 2.
———. "The Indianapolis Ghouls." Editorial. February 10, 1903, 4.
———. "Indianapolis Stirred Over the Desecration Of Graves." October 5, 1902, II, 10.
———. "In Dread Lest Their Dead Are in Dissecting Rooms." September 23, 1902, 6.
———. "Insanity of Cantrell Alleged…" February 10, 1903, 8.
———. "Insanity Plea." April 21, 1903, 1.
———. "Judge and Defendant Burned in Effigy." April 24, 1903, 5.
———. "King of Ghouls Granted Conditional Pardon…" May 2, 1909, I, 4.
———. "Lights Will Be Placed in the Cemeteries." October 13, 1902, 5.
———. "Local Ghouls at Noblesville…" March 13, 1903, 8.
———. "Louisville Doctor Signed Name…" March 25, 1903, 7.
———. "Louisville Reported to Have Received…" October 4, 1902, 9.
———. "Medical Colleges…" October 1, 1902, 7.
———. "More Ghouls Are to Be Arrested…" December 30, 1902, 8.
———. "More Sensations in Alexander Trial…" February 14, 1903, 9.
———. "More Warrants…" October 12, 1902, III, 1.
———. "Murder and Torture a Pastime…" August 10, 1903, 2.
———. "Murder but Pleasant Pastime…" August 13, 1903, 2.
———. "Murder Confessions by Cantrell…" July 14, 1903, 2.

———. "Mystery of Two Murders May Be Solved." July 15, 1903, 7.

———. "Negro Ghouls Refuse to Testify…" April 11, 1903, 6.

———. "None Found." October 10, 1902, 6.

———. "No Record Kept…" October 2, 1902, 3.

———. "No Release for Rufus Cantrell…" June 4, 1905, I, 7.

———. "Other Ghouls to Plead Guilty." April 29, 1903, 5.

———. "Physicians Indicted…" October 26, 1902, I, 6.

———. "Practical Plan to Detect Would-Be Despoilers of a Grave." October 23, 1902, 1.

———. "Robbery of Graves…" September 20, 1902, 5.

———. "Rufus Cantrell Dying." June 12, 1904, I, 6.

———. "Scandal Results from Ghoul Cantrell's Refusal to Testify." April 14, 1903, 1.

———. "A Scar on the Back…" November 13, 1902, 3.

———. "Sentenced for Killing a Chinaman." May 21, 1903, 9.

———. "Several Murders May Be Cleared Up…" July 12, 1903, III, 1.

———. "State Rests Its Case: Defense of Ghoul Cantrell…" April 22, 1903, 7.

———. "'Stiff' Bill." January 2, 1903, 2.

———. "Still More Murders Charged…" August 14, 1903, 4.

———. "Ten Bodies…" October 5, 1902, III, 1.

———. "Too Small." November 19, 1902, 3.

———. "Twenty Persons Indicted…" October 28, 1902, 4.

———. "White Ghoul." November 1, 1902, 1.

———. "Wholesale Grave Robberies Recalled…" February 7, 1903, 1.

———. "Women Embalmers…" October 31, 1902, 5.

Marion [OH] *Daily Star.* "A Climax Reached." September 30, 1902, 1.

———. "King of Ghouls Cantrill [sic] Will Not Appear Against the Grave Robbers at Indianapolis." January 7, 1903, 1.

New York Times. "Find Woman's Skeleton after 20 Years' Quest." April 27, 1920, 12.

Washington Post. "Held Her Prisoner For Days." December 26, 1915, 3.

MONSTERS AND GHOSTS

Monsters on the Loose

Louisville Courier-Journal. "An Indiana Ghost." February 19, 1889, 1.

———. "A Mysterious Howler." December 28, 1883, 5.

———. "Strange Animal." August 26, 1902, 6.

The Unseen Speak

Louisville Courier-Journal. "Hark from the Tomb." May 22, 1887, 11.

The Haunted Bennett House

Louisville Courier-Journal. "Agreed to Die." July 2, 1895, 1+.

———. "Snow-White Figure." August 13, 1897, 8.

———. "Three Caskets." July 3, 1895, 5.

The Hard-Luck Cripe Family

Louisville Courier-Journal. "House of Many Tragedies." January 18, 1905, 8.

———. "Over-Burdened with Tragedies…" September 10, 1905, IV, 1.

The Face at the Window

Louisville Courier-Journal. "A Face at the Window." December 14, 1891, 6.

Mrs. Freeman's Full House

Louisville Courier-Journal. "A Vincennes Ghost." January 28, 1888, 3.

A Gliding Ghost

Louisville Courier-Journal. "A Ghost Story." November 1, 1889, 4.

———. "A Ghost that Glides." February 25, 1888, 2.

A Haunted Hoosegow

Louisville Courier-Journal. "A Spook in Jail." September 2, 1889, 8.

TALES FROM THE TOMBS

Death, Be Not Boring

Arizona Republican [Phoenix]. "He Was a Joker." May 13, 1893, 1.

Brunvand, Jan Harold. *The Choking Doberman.* New York: W.W. Norton, 1984.

Indianapolis Journal. "Suicide of Young Actor at Gas City." December 20, 1903, I, 1.

Louisville Courier-Journal. "An Actor Commits Suicide on the Stage." December 20, 1903, I, 5.

———. "Attempts to Shave While Sound Asleep." December 20, 1906, 1.

———. "Barber Was Dying While Shaving Customer." February 14, 1911, 11.

———. "Body Forced Through Space of Five Inches." August 25, 1902, 1.

———. "Bugs in Her Ear." February 14, 1897, I, 9.

———. "By Nitro-Glycerine." October 4, 1895, 7.

———. "Charles Howard's Body Found Upright in Water." September 26, 1905, 4.

———. "A Dangerous Game." September 21, 1901, 7.

———. "Died on the Same Day." March 6, 1904, II, 8

——— "Dies in Belief He Lost Ox." June 26, 1903, 6.

———. "Dug His Grave Before Killing Himself." June 29, 1909, 1.

———. "False Death Notice Causes Real Death." April 9, 1907, 1.

———. "Fatal Play." April 25, 1902, 8.

———. "In Desperate Hurry to Kill Himself." July 15, 1905, 6.

———. "Indiana Woman Salted Her Husband…" April 25, 1902, 2.

———. "In Wife's View…" February 9, 1909, 7.
———. "A Medical Wonder." April 13, 1879, 3.
———. "New Method of Suicide." March 8, 1902, IV, 3.
———. "Penetrated His Brain." March 15, 1896, I, 8.
———. "Poe's Poetry Too Much…" January 8, 1911, I, 8.
———. "Poison on Wall Paper Kills Three Wives…" April 8, 1907, 3.
———."Staked His Life on a Card Game and Lost." September 21, 1904, 4.
———. "Suicide by Dynamite." December 15, 1897.
———. "Suicide's Grewsome [*sic*] Wish Is Gratified." June 8, 1911, 1.
———. "Tried to Eat Snakes." June 20, 1903, 2.
Washington [PA] *Reporter*. "A Suicide Almost Without Parallel…" June 21, 1876, 3.

A Smorgasbord of Skeletons

Brandon, Jim. *Weird America*. New York: Dutton, 1978.
Louisville Courier-Journal. "Digs Up Bones of Giants." December 29, 1902, 4.
———. "Five Skeletons Found in an Old House." July 21, 1905, 1.
———. "Found Handcuffed Skeleton Buried." May 7, 1901, 2.
———. "Gigantic Skeleton Found." November 9, 1902, I, 8.
———. "An Indiana Mystery." December 27, 1877, 4.
———. "A Samson Threw Him Overboard." May 19, 1901, I, 6.
———. "A Skeleton Found in a Tree." February 12, 1888, 4.
———. "Skeletons Under a Church." October 26, 1903, 2.

Libeling the Dead

Louisville Courier-Journal. "Attempt to Obtain Revenge May Be Costly." June 1, 1901, 2.
———. "Indiana Preacher Shows No Mercy for the Dead." July 16, 1901, 1.
———. "Miners Protest Against Preacher's Words." January 31, 1906, 3.

The Vengeful Epitaph

Louisville Courier-Journal. "Tombstone Tells His Infamy." May 2, 1901, 4.

You Can Take It with You

Louisville Courier-Journal. "Cigars in Shroud." September 14, 1914, 10.

———. "Little Girl Took Doll to Grave With Her." April 16, 1903, 7.

———. "Suicide." November 29, 1902, I, 3.

———. "Took Them with Him." March 4, 1903, 3.

Funeral Spoilers

Louisville Courier-Journal. "Alive in Coffin in a Cemetery Vault." March 22, 1905, 2.

———. "Arose from Bier and Called for Beer." May 24, 1905, 1.

———. "Attired for Burial." January 13, 1901, II, 4.

———. "Corpse Sat Up." February 14, 1903, 4.

———. "Disappointed the Undertaker." March 3, 1886, 5.

———. "He Was Really Dead." March 12, 1889, 3.

———. "No Grave for Her." June 14, 1879, 4.

———. "Not Dead." November 11, 1902, 6.

———. "Not Yet in a Coffin." January 24, 1895, 2.

———. "Rose from His Coffin." September 29, 1902, 3.

———. "A Singular Case." August 11, 1885, 5.

———. "Thought to Have Been Buried Alive." May 23, 1895, 3.

———. "Was He Buried Alive?" December 17, 1894, 6.

New Albany Evening Ledger. "Laid at Rest." January 24, 1895, 4.

Advance Warning

Louisville Courier-Journal. "Dreamed of Death." July 5, 1901, 5.

———. "Dreamed of Grim Reaper." July 25, 1905, 1.

———. "Foretold Her Death." March 19, 1913, 5.

———. "His Dream Came True." October 1, 1901, 2.
———. "Mother's Dream of Death Comes True." April 24, 1910, I, 3.

Peculiar Manifestations of Grief

Louisville Courier-Journal. "Home Deserted." October 30, 1902, 2.
———. "Old Man's Grief." August 25, 1898, 7.
———. "Returns to Guard Grave Where Sweetheart Rests." May 10, 1903, III, 2.

A Stand-Up Kind of Guy

Evansville Courier. "Dead Minister Stood Behind Pulpit…" February 21, 1904, 1.
Louisville Courier-Journal. "Corpse Stood Up Against Wall…" February 22, 1904, 2.

A Sensitive Fellow

Louisville Courier-Journal. "Buries Secret." October 18, 1905, 8.

A Hater of Pianos and Organs

Louisville Courier-Journal. "Bars Pianos from Legatee's Home." July 25, 1907, 8.

He Wrote His Own Epitaph

Louisville Courier-Journal. "Secret of a Tree." October 4, 1898, 8.

The Bachelor's Warning

Louisville Courier-Journal. "Bachelor's Epitaph Perpetual Warning." February 14, 1908, 1.

BURIED TREASURE

Louisville Courier-Journal. "Box of Gold." July 1, 1903, 7.
———. "Buried Treasure Box Found…" February 20, 1914, 10.

———. "Crock of Gold Found." November 24, 1913, 10.
———. "Indiana Farmer Plows Up $1,000 in Gold." March 28, 1907, 3.
———. "Indiana's Silver Mine." August 31, 1891, 6.
———. "Kettle of Gold." March 21, 1900, 5.
———. "Looking for Buried Treasure…" October 20, 1901, IV, 2.
———. "The Secret May Die with Him." August 25, 1892, 6.
———. "Skeleton with Gold Coins." July 19, 1908, I, 7.

Grave Robbers Galore

The Grave Robber's Comeuppance

Kentucky Gazette [Lexington, KY]. "Horror of Horrors." March 24, 1880, 3.

Proud of His Work

Louisville Courier-Journal. "His Skeleton to Be His Monument." December 30, 1894, 2.

Random Resurrectionist Recountings

Louisville Courier-Journal. "Deed of a Ghoul." August 13, 1893, 10.
———. "Fears Grave Robbers." June 4, 1912, 9.
———. "Ghouls." March 8, 1896, II, 8.
———. "Kept Vigil." October 4, 1898, 9.
———. "Maniac Dug Up Body of His Dead Child." May 19, 1903, 3.

Battle for the Bones

Louisville Courier-Journal. "Battle Between Brothers of Dead Minister and Four Ghouls." December 6, 1904, 6.

A Sister's Vigil

Louisville Courier-Journal. "Jesse Coe's Sister Guards His Grave." September 10, 1908, 1.

His Own Private Cemetery

Louisville Courier-Journal. "Cemetery of Three Acres on Farm…" July 15, 1902, 4.

The Deserted Medical School

Evansville Daily Courier. "Action at Last." February 26, 1885, 4.

———. "A Chapter of Horrors." Editorial. February 24, 1885, 2.

———. "Horror!" February 24, 1885, 4.

———. "That Horror." February 25, 1885, 4.

Louisville Courier-Journal. "A Deserted Dispensary." February 24, 1885, 2.

———. "Evansville Still Excited." February 25, 1889, 3.

LIFE IS LIKE THAT SOMETIMES

Oh, Rats

Pittsburgh Press. "The Rat Was His Jonah." February 28, 1887, 2.

Tracks in the Rock

Louisville Courier-Journal. "Franklin Notes." November 17, 1879, 3.

———. "Who Made Those Tracks?" November 11, 1879, 2.

Indiana's Skunk Farms

Louisville Courier-Journal. "Hoosier Farmers' Unique Methods…" November 5, 1901, 8.

———. "Mephitis Americana." August 4, 1879, 1.

Convicted by a Dream

Louisville Courier-Journal. "Convicted by a Ghost." May 28, 1888, 6.

The Heroic Newsboy

Chicago Tribune. "Newsboy Hero's Open Air Funeral Viewed by 15,000." October 21, 1912, 1+.

———. "Newsboy's Sacrifice to Live." October 22, 1912, 3.

———. "Plan Big Show in Chicago…" November 3, 1912, II, Part I, 5.

———. "Rugh Memorial Fund $300." October 23, 1912, 2.

———. "Rugh's Sacrifice Inspires Others." November 4, 1912, 10.

Louisville Courier-Journal. "All Gary Attends Funeral…" October 21, 1912, 2.

New Orleans Times-Picayune. "Boy Tramp Gives His Own Life…" October 19, 1912, 3.

Indiana Eccentrics

Louisville Courier-Journal. "Bachelor Who Has Unique Distinction in Indiana." April 7, 1904, 5.

———. "Building His Own Monument…" July 24, 1905, 10.

———. "Eccentric Indiana Man Dead." June 15, 1897, 2.

———. "End Seems Near." August 7, 1906, 5.

———. "For His Burial…" September 19, 1907, 7.

———. "On Verge of Lying in Grave Dug by Himself." January 19, 1905, 5.

———. "Steadily at Work on His Own Coffin." December 28, 1904, 6.

———. "Took Her Secret With Her." November 25, 1900, II, 6.

———. "Uncle Ike Perry Becomes Ninety-Five Years Old Today." October 29, 1905, I, 5.

———. "Wild Man at Large." September 10, 1899, 6.

———. "Wild Man Caught in Indiana." January 22, 1899, I, 6.

Love Fever

Louisville Courier-Journal. "Smallpox Has No Terrors for Lover…" April 19, 1902, 3.

He Took His Time

Louisville Courier-Journal. "Started After Cows Forty-Three Years Ago." March 17, 1910, 1.

Feats of Merrifield

Louisville Courier-Journal. "Blind Man's Feats." August 25, 1902, 2.

A Legal Conundrum

Louisville Courier-Journal. "Doctor Writes His Own Death Certificate." August 8, 1913, 10.

Men Have Killed for Less

Louisville Courier-Journal. "Convict Slays to Get Tobacco." August 22, 1913, 1.

———. "Murder Inquiry." August 23, 1913, 12.

The Jury System in Action

Louisville Courier-Journal. "Trouble May Come to Members of Indiana Jury." October 15, 1903, 3.

Is the Entrance to Hell in Indiana?

Louisville Courier-Journal. "Landing of Charon Is Found in Indiana?" January 29, 1905, V, 4.

A Horrid Disease

Louisville Courier-Journal. "Saved His Bones to Be Buried with Him." August 28, 1905, 8.

Marvelous Griffith

Louisville Courier-Journal. "Child's Play for Arthur F. Griffith…" February 18, 1906, I, 6.

———. "Indiana's Lightning Calculator Dies." December 26, 1911, 3.

New Orleans Times-Picayune. "Marvelous Griffith…" December 26, 1911, 1.

No Smoking Allowed

Louisville Courier-Journal. "Chimpanzee Died for Lack of Cigarettes." August 4, 1905, 8.

———. "Cigarette Smoke in the Air Again." April 28, 1906, 3.

———. "Doesn't Apply to Act of Smoking." April 27, 1906, 1.

———. "Gay Old Monk Must Have Cigarettes…" July 28, 1905, 2.

———. "The Indiana Cigarette Law." Editorial. April 28, 1906, 6.

———. "Must Serve 29 Days…" July 10, 1905, 2.

———. "No Clemency for Indiana Men…" October 3, 1905, 8.

———. "Sent to Jail for Forty-Seven Weeks." 11, 1905, 9.

———. "So Anxious to Smoke Cigarettes He Will Test the Law." May 13, 1905, 7.

———. "Why the Cigarette Law Was Passed." Editorial. May 12, 1905, 4.

Other Books by Keven McQueen

Biography/History

Cassius M. Clay, Freedom's Champion (Turner Publishing, 2001)

Offbeat Kentuckians: Legends to Lunatics (McClanahan Publishing, 2001)

More Offbeat Kentuckians (McClanahan Publishing, 2004)

Historical True Crime

Murder in Old Kentucky: True Crime Stories from the Bluegrass (McClanahan Publishing, 2006)

Cruelly Murdered: The Murder of Mary Magdalene Pitts and Other Kentucky True Crime Stories (Jesse Stuart Foundation, 2008)

Strange Tales of Crime and Murder in Southern Indiana (The History Press, 2009)

FOLKLORE/HISTORY

Forgotten Tales of Kentucky (The History Press, 2008)
The Kentucky Book of the Dead (The History Press, 2008)

For blogs, details about other books and silliness, check out KevenMcqueen.com.